Exploits
of a
Reluctant
(But Extremely
Goodlooking)
Hero

For my husband, Nick, and our three beautiful children, Hannah, Sophie and Sam

Text © 2007 Maureen Fergus

Kids Can Press acknowledges the financial support of the Government of Ontario, through the Ontario Media Development Corporation's Ontario Book Initiative; the Ontario Arts Council; the Canada Council for the Arts; and the Government of Canada, through the BPIDP, for our publishing activity.

Published in Canada by
Kids Can Press Ltd.
29 Birch Avenue
Toronto, ON M4V 1E2

Published in the U.S. by
Kids Can Press Ltd.
2250 Military Road
Tonawanda, NY 14150

www.kidscanpress.com

Edited by Sheila Barry
Designed by Céleste Gagnon
Printed and bound in Canada

CM 07 0 9 8 7 6 5 4 3 2 1
CM PA 07 0 9 8 7 6 5 4 3 2 1

Library and Archives Canada Cataloguing in Publication

Fergus, Maureen
    Exploits of a reluctant (but extremely goodlooking) hero / Maureen Fergus.

ISBN-13: 978-1-55453-024-3 (bound) ISBN-10: 1-55453-024-5 (bound)
ISBN-13: 978-1-55453-025-0 (pbk.) ISBN-10: 1-55453-025-3 (pbk.)

I. Title.

PS8611.E735E96 2007   jC813'.6   C2006-904465-1

Kids Can Press is a *l©rus*™ Entertainment company

Exploits
of a
Reluctant
(But Extremely Goodlooking)
Hero

Maureen Fergus

 KCP FICTION

I've tried to explain that it's his duty
as a man and a father to teach me the
finer points of lovemaking, but he just
says things like "I'm not sure" and
"Put down your mother's bra."

Today at school I told my best friend, Roger, that our grade 7 teacher, Mr. Unger, must have some sort of bizarre sensory input disorder, because although I've consistently demonstrated a complete lack of interest in his teaching style, he persists in trying to entice me with his crazy antics.

"What's more," I said, "when he wears that green cowboy hat of his, he looks exactly like Mr. Potato Head on a stick!"

Unfortunately, I failed to notice that Mr. Potato Head was standing right behind me until after I'd regaled Roger with my impersonation of a large, misshapen tuber on a stick trying to teach me geometry. I told Mr. Unger his feelings wouldn't get hurt so often if he stopped listening in on my private conversations. He hauled me to my feet and hustled me to the office. The secretary sent me to the principal, who passed me on to the guidance counselor. After taking two aspirins, the guidance counselor suggested that I start keeping a diary as a way to express opinions I absolutely cannot keep to myself.

"Diaries are for girls," I replied. "And did you forget about my genetically weak wrists?" I pointed out that I'd never be able to grip a pen for long enough to put my many opinions to paper. Then I laid my head on the table and sighed, "The ugly truth is that Mr. Unger discriminates against me because of my disability. Why else would he demonstrate such intolerance when my wrists give out during class and I succumb to the temptation of disruptive horseplay?"

Unfortunately, the guidance counselor refused to file a formal discrimination complaint on my behalf. Instead, she called my mother, who descended upon me the minute I got home from school.

"Here," she said, thrusting a tape recorder at me. "Try speaking your mind to this instead of to the various adult authority figures in your life." It sounded suspiciously like keeping a diary, but before I could protest, she added, "Many learned men keep journals. Think of it as a journal for the weak wristed." I was flattered that she thought of me as a learned man and promised to give her suggestion serious consideration, just as soon as I'd finished watching all my television programs. In response, she frog-marched me up to my room and ordered me not to come out until I'd recorded some learned thoughts.

I wonder if this is how Einstein started.

•••••

This evening before dinner I informed my mother that although I'd found her initial approach in the matter of the tape recorder pushy and rude, I'd decided to embrace the idea of my own free will. I pointed out that as the sole heir to my late grandfather's great Canadian plumbing fortune, I owe it to the world to someday write my memoirs.

"These tapes will provide insight into the sad life of a boy who should have grown up in luxury, but instead grew up in a rented duplex — all because his mother chose a penniless nobody over the family millions." I said her refusal to dump my father even after my grandmother cut them off without a cent was Movie of the Week material and added, "Spending my formative years watching you two eke out our miserable existence has given me a connection with the common man that most people of privilege never have. In a way, it would be almost selfish of me not to record my unique perspective."

Shockingly, my mother didn't offer a single word of encouragement even though the tape recorder had been her idea in the first place. Flinging another Salisbury steak into the deep fryer, she said I had as much connection with the common man as I did with the man in the moon, and that if I thought we had a miserable existence, I obviously didn't know the first thing about real poverty.

I waited in silence for a few moments, hoping she might apologize for her outburst. When she didn't, I quietly reminded her that I prefer my Salisbury steak barbecued, and left the room.

●●●●●

Today after school, while we were supposed to be studying for our math final, I showed Roger my tape recorder and let him listen to some of my musings. He waited until I went to the kitchen for more chocolate Ding Dongs, then recorded the sound of himself belching over top of a particularly insightful passage. I was very distressed when I discovered what he'd done and said, "You'd better shape up if you want any hope of being portrayed in a favorable light in my memoirs, buster!" In response, he belched again and asked if I wanted to see him stuff three chocolate Ding Dongs into his mouth at once.

I don't think I'll share my musings with Roger again. I get the feeling he doesn't completely grasp their significance.

●●●●●

My rich grandmother called from Florida this evening. She wanted to speak with my mother instead of listening to me go on and on about my memoirs. I could hardly believe it! Usually, she treats my mother like almost as much of a shunned outcast as my aunt Maud, who my grandmother believes purposely became a lesbian as a way to lash out at her. I once asked my aunt Maud about this and she said, "People don't choose to be homosexuals any more than they choose to have brown eyes. I was born a lesbian; aggravating your grandmother has just been a bonus."

More mysterious than the fact that my grandmother wanted to speak with my mother is the fact that my mother wanted to speak with her. They talked for almost an hour in the privacy of the den, and though I did my best to listen in, my mother can be surprisingly soft-spoken when she wants to be and I couldn't hear a thing.

• • • • •

My parents have been having many closed-door discussions these days. I'm sure it has something to do with the chain of plumbing retail outlets my grandfather founded, the House of Toilets, because I heard them talking about it again this morning while they were making breakfast. Intrigued, I tiptoed down the hall, burst into the kitchen and demanded clarification. My father was so startled that he knocked over the orange juice, but my mother just looked flustered and changed the subject.

• • • • •

This afternoon, while Roger and I were spying on my parents having another private discussion, they suddenly started necking. I was so horrified that it took me a minute to notice that Roger was enjoying the show. When I whispered, "What kind of a friend are you?" he just told me to shush and made me go get my Polaroid camera.

• • • • •

Tonight before bed I asked my mother flat out what she and my father have been talking about and she told me, "None of your business."

How rude.

• • • • •

I secretly called my grandmother and asked if *she* knew what my parents were hiding from me. She said, "I certainly do!" and proceeded to spill the beans.

Apparently, the management structure at the House of Toilets flagship store in Winnipeg is collapsing down around my grandmother's ears. The poor performance of this one store is dragging down the whole chain, and since my grandmother has no interest in returning to Winnipeg to run the business, her only hope of keeping my grandfather's legacy in the family is to get a family member to do it for her.

My aunt Maud has already refused to give up her thriving surgical practice for the privilege of taking over the House of Toilets and my grandmother says that aunt Maud's lesbian partner, Ruth, will run the business over her dead body. So that just leaves my parents and me.

I was stunned by the revelation. True, my personal fortune is in jeopardy, but after years of hardship, we are finally being called back to take our rightful place at the helm of the family empire. Hooray!

My mother came running when she heard me cheering. As soon as she figured out what I'd learned

— and from whom — she was pretty ticked off. After watching me leap for joy until I landed wrong and twisted my ankle, she urged me not to get too worked up.

"Your father and I didn't want to mention anything until we'd made a decision," she explained. "There are a lot of things to consider — my job, his job, the prospect of living under your grandmother's tyrannical thumb."

Massaging my wounded ankle, I suggested that they try thinking of someone other than themselves for a change — someone such as me, for example.

"We are thinking of you, honey. Money and power aren't everything, you know," she replied. "Your father and I have given you the greatest gift of all: a loving home where your spirit has the freedom to blossom." She said other things as well, but it was hard to hear them over the sound of my fake retching noises.

Freedom to blossom. Yech.

•••••

I told Roger the big news. He was stunned.

"You'll have to move," he said. "And go to a new school where you don't know anyone. What if they wear weird clothes or listen to freaky music?"

I replied that nearly every shirt I own is velour, so I wasn't worried about fitting in on the fashion front, and that I only listen to talk radio, so music wasn't really an issue, either. As for not knowing anyone, I said I was just going to be thankful to get away from Carmine Dinino, who that very afternoon had chased me into the girls' washroom after I reported him for writing unkind things about my manhood on the locker room wall.

After that, Roger could see the upside of moving, but he remained glum until I offered to fetch him another pack of Ding Dongs.

• • • • •

This morning over breakfast, I advised my mother that I was looking forward to being more than a figurehead at the House of Toilets.

"As the future owner of the company," I explained, "I want every little cog in my great organization to know that I am a man of action!"

After she stopped laughing, my mother confessed that I wasn't even being considered for a management position.

"If we do this at all," she said, "it'll be your father or me running the show."

When I pointed out that it was her job as a wife to stand by her man, not to trample all over him in search of personal glory, she started singing, "These Boots Were Made for Walkin'" and high-stepped it out of the room.

• • • • •

I told Roger about my mother's plan to squeeze me out of the House of Toilets. He pointed out that I was on the brink of failing grade 7 math, while my mother was at least a university graduate.

"What are you implying?" I demanded.

He shrugged and said he was implying that she probably knows more than I do about running a business. When I told him I'd never been so insulted in my entire life, he asked, "Not even when Carmine Dinino said that you sucked buffalo farts?"

 Tape #1

"Not even then!" I replied.

I guess I showed him exactly how insulted I was.

•••••

For days I've been pestering my parents about whether or not we're going to take over the House of Toilets. My mother has pretty well decided that her work as a public health nurse is too important to give up, but my father is warming up to the idea. He's been studying business at night school and feels that after eleven years as the produce manager at FoodBarn, he's just about exhausted opportunities for personal growth and development.

"This could be the challenge I've been waiting for," he said last night at dinner. "More importantly, saving the House of Toilets could be the first step on the road to mending fences with your grandmother."

After asking me to get my elbows out of my mashed potatoes, my mother added that a lot would depend on just how badly the store is performing.

"We're driving to Winnipeg next week to go over the books and meet with your grandmother, who is flying in from Florida," she said. "We'll know more after that."

•••••

This afternoon, when I told my mother that as a man of thirteen I felt perfectly comfortable looking after myself in their absence, she said that she'd already arranged for me to stay over at Roger's house. Given that Roger is my best friend, you'd think I'd be thrilled by the idea, but nothing could be further from the truth. Roger's bedroom hasn't seen the business end of a vacuum cleaner since the time his mother accidentally sucked up his tarantula, which had been nesting in a pile of dirty underwear and candy wrappers. He's not allowed to keep his pets in his room anymore, but I hardly think that's the point. The place is a public health hazard and I've never been comfortable wallowing in other people's filth. Perhaps I'll ask Mrs. Dodger to make up the guest bedroom for me.

• • • • •

So far, life at Roger's has been every bit as harrowing as I had anticipated. Mrs. Dodger thought I was joking when I asked her to make up the guest bedroom for me, so I spent last night huddled in my sleeping bag, waiting for Roger's jockstrap to drop from the light fixture and hit me in the face. Then, today after school, I snuck what I thought was a chocolate pudding cup out of Roger's fridge and nearly had a heart attack when I discovered it was crammed full of dead mice.

"It's Cup o' Mice," explained Roger, helping me up off the floor. "Dinner for George."

"Who is George?" I asked in a near-hysterical voice.

"My corn snake," whispered Roger, who hesitated before confiding, "He's been missing since Monday."

• • • • •

When my parents called this evening to say good-night to me, they let it slip that the House of Toilets is in much worse shape than my grandmother realized. It seems the neighborhood in which the store is located has really deteriorated over the last couple of years and this has driven off a lot of customers. The decrease in sales has required the manager to cut salaries, which has resulted in the loss of experienced staff and left the place in a shambles. My father thinks he could do great things with the store, but after reviewing the financials, my mother is not at all keen to take the risk.

"After all," she pointed out, "we both have good jobs in Regina, and a bird in the hand is worth two in the bush."

Before hanging up, I told them about George and the jockstrap and asked them to...

AHHHH! ROGER! ROGER! I SEE GEORGE! HE'S IN THE BATHROOM — HE'S COMING FOR ME, ROGER AND ... OH, NO — WAIT A MINUTE — IT'S JUST THE BELT OF YOUR FATHER'S BATHROBE ... WHAT? ... I CAN'T HEAR YOU, MRS. DODGER — SPEAK UP. WHY ARE YOU WHISPERING? ... OH! Well, yes, as a matter of fact, I CAN stop screaming before I wake up the whole house.

... hurry home before I am scarred for life.

•••••

My parents got back from Winnipeg, and I'm sad to say that they're still at odds regarding the House of Toilets opportunity. My father is more eager than ever to prove himself to my grandmother, who collapsed in a heap complaining of chest pains when he floated the idea that he take over the store. However, my mother doesn't want to see him get into a no-win situation, particularly when inventory mismanagement and poor accounts collection have left the business in such a tenuous position relative to cash flow. Personally, I think she's just jealous that my father can be so decisive while she continues to waffle.

On a positive note, my mother found George when she was unpacking my overnight bag. Not only is Roger relieved to have him back again, but I found her reaction to the sight of a three-foot corn snake tangled in my bathing trunks highly entertaining.

•••••

I've informed my mother that I think she needs to work at rekindling the youthful spontaneity that caused her to elope to Grand Forks fourteen years ago with a man she hardly knew when she wasn't even pregnant. I said, "Your reluctance to throw caution to the wind and jump into the House of Toilets with both feet is really making you seem frumpy and middle-aged." I felt this little speech might be the exact jolt she needed to make her lay off with her constant yammering about the pros and cons of taking over the business. Instead, she made a crabby face and said, "Maybe if you pay attention you'll learn something."

"The only thing I'm learning is that you can be a real drag sometimes," I replied.

After that, she sent me to my room.

You see what I mean about her being a drag sometimes.

•••••

This afternoon, Mr. Unger handed back our final math tests. Afterward, once the class settled into some self-directed study I had no interest in, I went up to his desk, explained that I didn't feel my mark reflected my enormous intellectual potential and said that I'd appreciate having it bumped up to a D minus. He refused and pointed out that since I never paid attention in class or completed my homework, my poor performance shouldn't come as a complete shock.

"Well, it does," I admitted. Then I asked if I could go lie down in the nurse's office until the feeling passed. When he said no, I collapsed on his desk in order to demonstrate how sincerely shocked I was, but he was too busy mopping up his spilled coffee to pay much attention.

• • • • •

Due to government cutbacks, my mother has been unexpectedly laid off from her job as a public health nurse. She is devastated, and of course I feel terrible for her, but what terrific timing for my father and me! From now on, she will only spend day after empty day sitting at home watching television, so what difference does it make whether she does it here or in Winnipeg?

• • • • •

As I predicted, when I got home from school today, my mother was lying on the couch watching *The Oprah Winfrey Show*. She was also eating a big bag of Cheez Doodles, so to be funny and cheer her up, I sang out, "A moment on the lips, a lifetime on the hips!" In response, she threw an empty diet cola can in my direction and told me to go get her another one from the fridge.

She is going to make a very unpleasant shut-in.

• • • • •

My aunt Maud called this evening to commiserate with my mother. From what I could tell, the two of them mostly discussed what a bunch of pinheads the bozos who run the provincial government are for cutting community-based health programs that actually make a difference in the long run. My mother blazed, "You're absolutely right, Maudy. There *will* be tremendous consequences to this kind of shortsighted policy decision!"

Later, my father brought my mother some peppermint tea in bed and missed the better part of a M*A*S*H rerun listening to her jabber on about her conversation with Aunt Maud. It would have put me into a coma, but he said things like "I couldn't agree more!," "What an excellent point!" and "How about a foot rub, sweetheart?"

After hearing that, I couldn't bear to listen any longer, so I stopped pressing my ear against their bedroom door and went to bed.

● ● ● ● ●

Thanks to her family's loving support, my mother is back to her aggressive, opinionated old self. She says that losing her job isn't the end of the world and that it's time she stopped feeling sorry for herself. I said, "I couldn't agree more," and pointed out that no one likes a complainer.

"You should know!" she retorted. Then she had a good, long laugh at my expense. I'm sure I don't know what that's supposed to mean. I never complain unless something's bothering me, and I just happen to be more sensitive about most things than most people. Just because a person is sensitive is no reason to laugh at him.

My mother also says that since she's going to have to start over anyway, she might as well do it in Winnipeg.

"I still have some reservations about the viability of the flagship store and about my mother's ability to keep her nose out of things," she admitted, "but this seems very important to your father. Besides, the worst that can happen is the worst that can happen."

I suggested that she tone down her enthusiasm or "Up With People" might snatch her away in the night, but she just laughed and snapped her gum at me.

I was being sarcastic, of course. I don't really think "Up With People" would snatch her away in the night, and if they did, they'd probably return her in a big hurry. She's not the kind of person who mixes well with the free-love crowd.

• • • • •

Today, I informed my classmates that I would be leaving Regina forever. I could tell from the loud, sustained applause that they were happy for my good fortune — all except Carmine Dinino. He told me, "Good riddance," and made several rude gestures involving his crotch, which I reported to Mr. Unger. As he was being dragged to the office, I tried to stress to Carmine that he brought these things upon himself, but he shook his fist at me in such a violent fashion that I dropped the subject.

Sometimes you've got to quit while you're ahead.

• • • • •

My father has given notice at the FoodBarn. Everyone is sad to see him go, except for his boss, Johnny O'Piglet, who's had it in for my father ever since he made up the nickname "O'Piglet" and accidentally mentioned it to everyone in the store.

• • • • •

School is over and I have to admit I'm disappointed the class didn't throw me a going-away party. However,

Mr. Unger did take me aside and say that he knew I had it in me to grow up to be a decent human being if I really put my mind to it.

I am touched. Mr. Unger and I haven't gotten along that well this year, and I think it was big of him to admit I have potential.

•••••

This evening, one of the old ladies who regularly trolls the produce department at FoodBarn came by the store with a plateful of cookies and a card that said, "Farewell, Fruit Boy." My father was terribly moved — he has always maintained that his job is about customer service, not fruit, and that this is why it has remained a challenge after all these years.

All I have to say is that he must be pretty secure in his masculinity to let people refer to him as "Fruit Boy." In case he hasn't noticed, he is well over thirty years old.

•••••

Even though Roger and I had planned to spend the entire summer at the outdoor municipal pool checking out the bathing beauties, Mrs. Dodger insisted that Roger accompany the family to Disney World, so I've spent the last three weeks alone, wandering listlessly from room to room, rifling through the boxes that my mother has so carefully packed in preparation for our move to Winnipeg. She says that if I don't stop making a nuisance of myself she's going to find something productive for me to do, but I think we both know she's bluffing.

•••••

Oh, horrors! My mother has volunteered my services to the community center's summer drop-in program until the last of our boxes is loaded onto the moving van.

"But why?" I cried, waving a set of brass candlesticks at her. Instead of answering, she snatched the candlesticks from me, rewrapped them in newspaper and ordered me out of the room.

• • • • •

Kevin, the drop-in program coordinator, has put me in charge of the paste station. This is not as much of a coup as it might seem — the stuff tastes just as revolting now as it ever did. This is going to be a long few weeks.

• • • • •

Roger returned from Disney World with a pair of souvenir mouse ears for me, and many exciting stories about rides that would make me vomit. I pleaded with him to consider becoming my assistant at the paste station, but he refused on the grounds that there would be no bathing beauties to ogle. He had me there.

• • • • •

On my way home from the community center today, I visited the Regina House of Toilets to let the local yokels know that we'll be leaving town any day now. It was difficult to gauge the level of their disappointment, because they did a lot of smiling and congratulating me on my good fortune, but I know they must be taking it hard. It isn't often that country bumpkins in a nationwide chain get the opportunity to rub shoulders with the future owner of the company.

• • • • •

My aunt Maud's partner, Ruth, has pulled together a small selection of rental properties for us to choose from when we arrive in Winnipeg. In addition to being a radical left-wing social activist, Ruth is a real estate agent, and I've given her a long list of the features I'd like to see in our next home, including a luxurious private bathroom for me and central vacuum for my mother. Ruth expressed surprise, but I said, "I'm not always thinking only of myself, you know." I also said that if she needs to prioritize, the luxurious private bathroom should come before the central vac. She said she'd take it under advisement. She is a good woman that way.

• • • • •

I've watched television and eaten Ding Dongs with Roger for the last time. We had a sleepover last night, and after we finished making crank calls to Mr. Unger and wrestling over the Polaroids Roger took of my parents necking, we sat on the back stoop and made empty promises about keeping in touch.

I will miss Roger. He's been a good pal.

• • • • •

The drive to Winnipeg was long and boring and I complained incessantly. There was plenty to complain about, including the fact that my mother made me play "I Spy" every time I complained, which was about as much fun as a pin in the eye.

We've been staying at the Royal Victoria Motor Hotel since we arrived in the city. I've been getting up early every morning and stealing "Do Not Disturb" signs in the hopes that maids will burst in on guests fornicating. Every afternoon I've been practicing my running cannon-balls until I get kicked out of the pool by the manager. For a while, I was also hanging out with a swim team from Calgary, but none of them have spoken to me since yesterday after lunch, when I landed on one of their members while I was doing my running cannonballs.

That's okay with me, though. All their girls smell like chlorine.

●●●●●

Aunt Maud and Ruth gave us a real "Friendly Manitoba" welcome tonight. Ruth had told us to swing by their place for some Chinese takeout after Aunt Maud got home from the hospital. The minute we stepped into their tastefully decorated foyer, however, three dozen lesbians we'd never set on eyes on before shouted, "WELCOME TO WINNIPEG!" right in our faces. My father was so startled that his arm shot out and knocked over a large, expensive-looking vase. It landed right in front of my mother, who tripped over it and tore yet another hole in her favorite old track pants. I said, "Does this mean no pork balls for dinner?" In response, Aunt Maud directed me to the dining room, where the caterers were laying out a first-class feast in our honor.

Tomorrow, we're going to pick out a rental property. After the star treatment we got tonight, I can't wait to see what Ruth has in store for us!

●●●●●

Ruth's selection of houses didn't include even one with a luxurious private bathroom for me. I was so disappointed. When I told her I thought she'd done a pretty poor job following my instructions, she went off on a tirade about how I should be grateful for all I have in a world where so many have so little. I can definitely see why morally indignant people are so unpopular sometimes. Personally, I'd like to be a liberal-minded activist someday, but only if I can keep with the conservative mainstream. I don't see the point of moral indignation if it gets you labeled a social outcast. Who does that help?

Anyway, my parents selected a house not far from the House of Toilets because my father feels that since he's the manager of a local business, his family should become part of the community. I said, "Who do you think you are? The Godfather?" and begged him to reconsider renting among the wealthy. When he refused, I asked, "Does this mean you're not going to enroll me in an exclusive private school, either?" He confirmed that I would still be attending public school.

Public school! It is worse than I thought.

•••••

I've taken a walking tour of the neighborhood. Besides the House of Toilets, there is a café, a gas station, a strip mall, a hotel and lounge, a 7-Eleven, a liquor store, a soup kitchen, two discount clothing outlets and a pawnshop, where I've just learned that I can get cash in exchange for a variety of common household items my mother would probably never notice are missing.

This may not be as bad as I first anticipated.

•••••

This morning, while my mother was taking a shower, I put the blender, the hand mixer and the slow cooker into my knapsack and hurried up to Felix's Pawnshop. Unfortunately, Felix refused to take them without a note from my mother, even after I gave him my solemn word of honor that I had permission to sell them.

It is hard to believe that solemn words of honor don't carry more weight in this world.

•••••

We visited the House of Toilets flagship store for the first time today. While my father met with senior staff, I did my customary walk-through. The sales people stared as I strolled among them pointing out displays that needed dusting, and I was privately amused by their awestruck reaction, until one of them pointed out that I had toilet paper hanging out the back of my pants.

Later, when my grandmother called to give my father more tips on how to achieve the aggressive sales targets she has set for him, I complained about this lack of respect.

"Results are more important than respect," she said. "You can't take respect to the bank."

"You can't take barbecued beef ribs to the bank either," I replied, "but they're still high on my list of priorities."

She chortled at this and called me a whipper-snapper, then promised me ribs the next time she's in town.

● ● ● ● ●

School is only days away, and this afternoon, after she finished buying me school supplies and couple of new velour shirts, my mother drove me past my new school. It looks much larger than my old one, and I'm sure I would have found it very intimidating if I weren't so confident about my ability to excel in everything except schoolwork and athletic endeavors.

I wonder how less-gifted students cope with the pressure of changing schools.

● ● ● ● ●

I started school today. My new teacher's name is Miss Thorvaldson and she is obviously a fashion plate, because she was wearing knee-high boots with three-inch heels, a double string of pearls and a black knit sweater dress that left practically nothing to the imagination. This wasn't nearly as thrilling as you might think, however, because she is also the most obese woman I have ever laid eyes on. In fact, I was so startled by her size that all I could do was gape in amazement until she gave me a nasty look and ordered me to my seat.

I share a desk with a girl named Missy Shoemaker who told me to bugger off when I said that I hoped she wasn't one of those know-it-all girls who would rather get good grades than be popular with the boys, and I sit right in front of a brute named Lyle Filbender, whom I caught picking his nose during Social Studies. When he grunted, "What're you looking at, buttwad?" I gave his index finger a meaningful glance. He responded by flicking his booger at me. If this behavior continues, I will have no choice but to report him. Boogers are extremely unsanitary business.

Besides me, there's only one other new kid in the class. His name is John Michael Sweetgrass, and he just transferred over from Niji Mahkwa, a school that specifically caters to the Native Canadian crowd. He transferred because he was tired of having to take the bus to school. Over lunch, I said, "You're crazy," and told him I'd do just about anything to get out of walking to school. Then I offered to trade half my revolting egg salad sandwich for two of his delicious cream puff pastries, and he accepted.

This could be the start of a beautiful friendship.

•••••

I've just learned that we will be receiving instruction in Family Life this year. That's just another name for Sex Education, and I'm looking forward to it. Puberty is right around the corner, and my father has done a pretty poor job of my at-home instruction. He does a great deal of waffling on subjects such as the best way to get a girl to lift up her shirt, because he says he doesn't think he should be telling me things like that. I've tried to explain that it's his duty as a man and a father to teach me the finer points of lovemaking, but he just says things like "I'm not sure" and "Put down your mother's bra."

I hope my Family Life teacher won't be so quick to throw away teachable moments.

•••••

Of all the coincidences — John Michael lives just down the street from me, and his mother works at the Blue Moon Café, which just happens to make the delicious cream puff pastries that I so thoroughly enjoyed at lunch the other day! When I told John Michael that this put him in a very good position to take over as my new best friend, he seemed pleased.

•••••

John Michael had kickboxing lessons after school today, so instead of walking home with him, I wandered over to 7-Eleven to agonize over what candy to buy with my measly allowance. After being asked to leave the store for sniffing the Lik-M-Aid too closely, I bumped into the manager of the Holy Light Mission. His name is Jerry, and he was handing out free Cheez Whiz sandwiches to the people hanging around the empty lot beside the Mission. I introduced myself and told him that I prefer cold cuts. Then I said, "Handing out free sandwiches is no way to run a business, my friend."

Jerry laughed and explained that it was his job to feed the hungry. I watched an old woman in a limp blue toque shove half a sandwich into the pocket of her filthy overcoat and told Jerry that he must have the worst job in the whole world.

"On the contrary," he replied. "It's a privilege to serve my fellow man."

He told me I should try it sometime; I explained that I had my hands full just looking after my own interests, wished him luck and continued on my way.

• • • • •

This afternoon I met Marv, the owner of the gas station on the corner, when I burst into his establishment shouting for a bathroom because my Super Big Gulp had passed through me faster than anticipated and I wasn't sure I could make it home without having an accident.

"Bathrooms are for paying customers," he grouched, launching into a big, sad story about how people like me are always hanging around his place driving off paying customers. In desperation, I cried, "If you don't let me use the bathroom immediately, I may very well urinate all over your floor!" I urged him to consider how many paying customers *that* would drive off, but he just said, "Sorry. If I bend the rules for you, I've got to bend them for everyone."

What a ludicrous statement. When will people learn

that giving me preferential treatment doesn't give anyone else the right to expect it?

●●●●●

This evening after dinner, I accompanied my father back to the House of Toilets. He's been working late almost every night, and my mother wanted me to make sure that he got home at a decent hour for once. I had hoped to use the time to clear up a few things, but before I'd finished asking him even one of the many long, distracting questions that had been plaguing me since dinner, my father suggested I go exploring. I headed directly for the office of the assistant manager. I spent almost fifteen minutes going through his private papers and exploring the contents of his desk, but found nothing interesting until I was leaving, when I spotted a locked metal box lying hidden in the potted palm by the door. I gave it a shake and it jingled like a treasure box! I immediately searched every inch of it for a tag or a sticker or some other indication of ownership. Finding nothing — not even a scratch! — I concluded that this was an open-and-shut case of Finders Keepers. Excitedly, I stuffed the box under my jacket.

Later, in the privacy of my bedroom, I pried it open with a screwdriver. It was filled with money — more than nine hundred dollars! I gathered the bills into a big wad and stuffed it into the back pocket of my GWG Scrubbies. It's not the best look for my buns, but I can definitely afford to let my looks go a little now. Rich men are always popular, even ugly ones, like Donald Trump. I only hope I won't have to spend much on my lackeys and bimbos, because greed is a pretty insincere basis for a friendship. I want to be a popular rich guy, but I want people to love me for more than my money.

•••••

I told John Michael about my newfound wealth. Instead of showing mindless joy for me, he expressed concern over the fact that I'd stolen something from the assistant manager's office. Feeling huffy, I pointed out that finding something half buried in the dirt is practically the same as finding it in the garbage and that if the box had meant so much to its owner, he would have put his name on it.

"Would *you* leave nine hundred dollars lying around in an unmarked box?" I asked.

Just as John Michael opened his mouth to offer what could only have been a heartfelt apology for doubting my integrity, Miss Thorvaldson asked me to kindly return to my own seat and stop talking during the announcements. I said, "In a minute," and tried to return to my conversation with John Michael, but she interrupted me again and again and finally dragged me down the aisle by the arm and put me into my seat.

•••••

Ughhhh ... I've been spending large amounts of money on candy these past few days and have developed several horrendously painful canker sores. The manager at 7-Eleven said he's never seen anyone eat so much Lik-M-Aid in his life, but I told him it was really none of his business. Boy, you throw a little money around and suddenly everybody has an opinion.

Unfortunately, I haven't yet seen a surge in my popularity. I was hoping that people would be able to sense my wealth, but it looks like I'm going to have to grease some wheels. I already feel used.

•••••

I handed out fifty dollars to the street people at the Holy Light Mission. There were tears of joy. Admittedly, it's not the best crowd to be popular with, but I figured I could get them for cheap. Jerry was very surprised.

"Where did you get all that money?" he asked. "And are you sure your parents don't mind that you're giving it away?"

In response to both questions, I just laughed and peeled off a fiver.

• • • • •

My mother thinks I must be ill because I've barely been touching my dinner these days. This is because I've been secretly sneaking to Totally Fried Chicken after school and ordering four-piece chicken dinners with coleslaw and large fries. I haven't told her that, though. Instead, I've taken the opportunity to comment that I haven't been finding her meals all that palatable and to suggest that if she reduces the Beefaroni content in our diet, my appetite might be enticed back. She hasn't responded positively yet, but I am hoping.

This evening I calculated that I have enough money left to order one hundred and twelve more four-piece chicken dinners, as long as I don't give any more money to charity. Time to tighten the belt, I guess. Too bad for Jerry's street people.

• • • • •

I haven't yet told my parents about my generosity at the Holy Light Mission. I'm hoping that they'll learn of it from one of my beneficiaries. That way, I will not only look kind and generous but humble, as well. I can't wait for them to find out. I will be a hero!

• • • • •

There has been a theft at the House of Toilets. Our petty cash has been stolen! Petty cash is the loose change that a business keeps handy to pay incidental business expenses. The assistant manager says that he always keeps it in a locked metal box on the top shelf of the bookcase in his office, but that today when he went to pay the courier, the box was gone! I thought about mentioning the locked metal box I found but decided it was just a distracting coincidence. After all, I found my locked metal box in the potted palm — a far cry from the bookcase. John Michael says I'm splitting hairs, but I've decided to ignore him for the sake of our friendship.

• • • • •

Missy Shoemaker has requested a new desk mate on account of my flatulence. I am humiliated. It must be the Totally Fried Chicken — perhaps some chemical in the krispy koating is not agreeing with me. I've tried to reason with Missy, but she says that I smell like a dead prairie dog caught in a heating duct.

I think it is safe to say that being popular with the boys isn't high on her list of priorities.

• • • • •

A member of the cleaning staff has confessed to bumping the assistant manager's bookcase with her vacuum cleaner one evening last week, causing a locked metal box to fall from the top shelf. She tearfully explained that she was going to put it back, but just as she picked it up, she heard my father and me coming, and she panicked. Apparently, she'd been fired from her last job after being falsely accused of stealing, and since she badly needed this job, she decided to dump the important-looking box into the potted palm so that we wouldn't catch her holding it and jump to the wrong conclusion.

I now realize that there's a good chance my locked metal box is the one that everybody is looking for. It's obviously too late to make amends, however, so I've been continuing to secretly gorge myself on fried chicken. Also, since I don't want the poor cleaning lady to take the fall for something I did, I've been pointing out that, to be fair, all thirty-two House of Toilets employees should be on the suspect list. I even told my mother, "Any one of them could have pried that little triangular lock open with a screwdriver."

She gave me a strange look, but I'm sure it got her thinking.

•••••

Since I'm no longer keen to have my parents find out about the money I gave to Jerry's street people, I've been quietly asking them to keep their accolades to themselves. Many have said things like "Who are you?" and "What's an accolade?" in order to communicate that they're willing to pretend they don't remember me, so I think I'm okay.

Man, I fork out fifty bucks to the homeless and can't even bask in the recognition of my selfless act of kindness. What a waste.

•••••

Worst luck! I was walking down the street with my mother and we bumped into Jerry, who mentioned the fifty bucks and said he was sure that God had a special place in heaven for people like me.

In a loud voice, I replied that he must have me

confused with someone else, then I whispered to my mother that we should be careful, because this wacko was obviously having drug-induced hallucinations. She ignored me and told Jerry she was glad we could help. She didn't even sound mad! I was very relieved. Jerry invited us to drop by the Mission anytime.

"Don't forget to bring your wallet!" he added, laughing. I laughed, too, and pretended to write him a big, fat IOU. This made him laugh even harder, and he was still laughing as he waved good-bye.

I was still laughing as we walked away, but then my mother cuffed me on the back of the head and told me to zipper up. She accused me of stealing the petty cash box from the House of Toilets and trying to blame it on the employees. I shouted, "You've got no proof!" and ranted about injustice until she asked where I'd got the fifty dollars, at which point I broke down and confessed everything. I acted as contrite as I possibly could, while at the same time pointing out that only a person with a heart of stone would be unmoved by the fact that I'd given a portion of the stolen money to charity. My mother told me to stuff a sock in it. She also told me that I was going to volunteer at the Holy Light Mission for one morning every weekend until Christmas.

"That'll teach you what giving is all about," she fumed, dragging me down the sidewalk by the collar of my snazzy yellow windbreaker.

• • • • •

I returned the remaining petty cash to my mother, and she was shocked to discover that there was almost seven hundred dollars left. "I can't imagine what the assistant manager was thinking, having this much money on hand!" she exclaimed. She was really working up a head of steam, so, in order to increase her fury toward the assistant manager — and divert attention away from me — I said, "No kidding!" and explained that there had been well over nine hundred dollars to start with!

At first, she didn't believe I'd spent almost a hundred and fifty dollars on nothing but junk food, but then I showed her the big bag of empty Lik-M-Aid packages in my closet and explained about my daily sojourns to Totally Fried Chicken. After that, she believed me, but she didn't seem any less angry.

Boy. There is no pleasing some people.

•••••

I called John Michael tonight to tell him the sad news about how Jerry's big mouth had landed me in hot water. He said, "Bummer," and asked if this meant I wouldn't be playing weekend street hockey with him anymore.

"I was never going to play with you again, anyway," I confessed. "Last time, you hammered me with your pulverizing slap shot until I was nothing but a large, moaning bruise, remember?"

John Michael made a pleased noise and asked, "Do you really think I have a pulverizing slap shot?"

"I really do," I replied. Then I tried to talk some more about my sad news, but he said he had to go practice his stickhandling and hung up on me.

•••••

Missy Shoemaker claims I still stink.

"Impossible!" I cried in dismay, watching her scooch to the farthest edge of our still-shared desk. "I haven't had a bite of fried chicken in almost three days!"

Later, during music class, it occurred to me that I might be suffering the symptoms of withdrawal.

"Have a heart," I whispered to Missy. "It's a medical condition, just like the flatulence."

In response, she clanged a cowbell in my face and marched away.

• • • • •

I had hoped to get out of volunteering at the Mission by suggesting to Jerry that he repay my previous generosity by letting me off the hook without telling my mother, but no such luck.

"God would never forgive me if I let a pair of strong hands go to waste," he said. I explained that I was an atheist and so, in my books, there would be no harm done, but he just laughed and sent me to help the kitchen women cut up vegetables.

Later, I had to help serve because Jerry said it was important to get frontline experience. Everyone got one bowl of soup, one bun and one piece of fruit. The soup was thin, the buns were stale and the fruit had seen better days, but Jerry said, "The food is donated — we're lucky to get anything at all." He also said it was probably the best meal a lot of these people had had all week. I found that hard to believe. Most of them weren't even wearing ragged clothing, and if you have enough money to clothe yourself, how can you not have enough money to feed yourself? Jerry tried to tell me that poverty was complicated, but I think he was just covering up his amazement that I was able to offer such insight after only a few hours on the job.

• • • • •

In addition to making me work at the Mission to learn what giving is all about, my mother is forcing me to get a paper route in order to learn the value of money. What a drag! I've repeatedly told her that I know perfectly well how valuable money is, but she says that anyone who feels it appropriate to spend one hundred and fifty dollars on Lik-M-Aid and fried chicken obviously has no idea how much money that is.

A paper route! That is backbreaking labor, and I know for a fact that paperboys make some pretty measly cash. I will have to work very, very hard for every dollar I earn. You would think my mother could have come up with a better job than that if she wanted to teach me a lesson. I will never understand her logic.

• • • • •

My paper route started at five-thirty this morning. I am weak with exhaustion. My bag was so heavy that twice I dropped it in agony, and once I lost my balance and put my fist through a screen door. I also suffered a severe scrape to the face while taking a shortcut through someone's decorative hedge and wrenched my shoulder flinging the papers across the lawns of my last few customers.

When I finally dragged myself up the front steps, my mother was waiting with a mug of hot chocolate, but I stalked past her without drinking it because I thought I detected a hint of smugness in her warm smile. Later — feeling resentful that I'd missed out on a perfectly good mug of hot chocolate because of her — I pretended to be deaf when she wished me a pleasant day at school and I left the house without allowing her to kiss me good-bye.

I can't understand it. Overnight, my mother seems to have lost her ability to relate to me. She's going to have to work a little harder if she expects us to get along.

• • • • •

It was so cold this morning when I woke up that I felt sure I wouldn't be required to deliver papers. My mother agreed, but suggested that I go check if they'd been dropped off, just in case. "If they haven't," she said, "you can come home and I'll personally tuck you back into bed."

Filled with excitement, I ran all the way to the top of the street, only to discover that those overlords at the *Winnipeg Daily News* were right on schedule. Defeated, I lay down on the sidewalk and dreamed about how horrible my mother was going to feel when they found my frozen carcass. Then my feet started getting cold, so I stood back up and gathered my burden. My mother made me hot chocolate again this morning, and also chocolate chip muffins from a mix, but I've decided never to forgive her for this.

● ● ● ● ●

This afternoon, as the rest of the class was lining up for gym, I asked Miss Thorvaldson if I could be excused from participating in order to rest my aching shoulders. No sooner had I finished describing the unspeakable agony of carrying forty papers at once than Missy Shoemaker announced that she had a double route and carried eighty, no problem. In a whisper, she added, "What are you, a wimp?" so, with as much dignity as I could muster, I withdrew my request to be excused from gym class and took my place in line.

If she keeps this up, Missy Shoemaker will probably never get married.

● ● ● ● ●

Miss Thorvaldson hasn't been warming up to me the way I'd hoped, so I've been attempting to get on her good side

through the use of a few well-placed compliments. I've been trying to be especially flattering about her appearance. She's always dressed to the nines, so it's obviously important to her, and since large women almost never get complimented on their looks, I was sure this strategy would guarantee me a special place in her heart.

I thought it was working well until today after school, when I mentioned that I know a lot of men who prefer full-figured women. Miss Thorvaldson looked so startled by this revelation that I put my hand on hers and murmured that she could get emotional in front of me if she needed to. In response, she snatched her hand away and sent me to the office.

I hope this doesn't wipe out all the goodwill I've built up through my previous flattery. I just can't understand what went wrong! Perhaps it was my delivery — it's possible that I sounded insincere, since I don't actually know any men who prefer full-figured women. I, myself, don't feel the least bit aroused by them, even if they do have the biggest breasts.

● ● ● ● ●

I've put in a call to my aunt Maud to ask her advice about how to get my relationship with Miss Thorvaldson back on track. Ruth is far too touchy for me to trust her opinions on such a delicate matter, and I just know my parents would find some way to twist my words against me.

● ● ● ● ●

I attended a demonstration with Ruth on the weekend because my aunt Maud was busy in surgery, and also because Ruth promised to buy me as many Mr. Juicy hot dogs as I could eat and there is no finer boiled wiener in the city. I ate four, wandered over to the front lawn of the legislature to shout insults at the members of parliament and their mothers, then headed back to Mr. Juicy, where I was interviewed by the beautiful Lori Anderson of CTY television. When she said it was unusual to see a boy my age demonstrating with the Gay Women for Social Responsibility, I looked straight into the camera and said, "I'm proud to stand with my sisters." Then I shook my fist and shouted, "Down with government!" but I think they'd already turned the camera off by then.

● ● ● ● ●

A few kids at school saw my television interview with the beautiful Lori Anderson. Janine Schultz — who has an enormous crush on me and will say almost anything to worm her way into my affections — said that I spoke very well. Lyle Filbender called me a fairy. I said I wasn't the fairy, he was the fairy, and he picked his nose, as well. So he said I smelled like a horse's rear end, and I called him a pockmarked crater face, and so on and so forth, until finally he tried to stab me in the neck with a pencil. At that point, I reported the situation to Miss Thorvaldson, because I didn't want either of us to do something we might regret. Miss Thorvaldson gave us both detention, and later, Lyle taped a note to my locker that said, "YOUR DEAD!"

I may ask Trish, the school secretary, if I can have a peek at Lyle Filbender's file. I'm concerned that he may have a violent past.

● ● ● ● ●

After four straight days in surgery, my aunt Maud finally returned my call concerning my relationship

with Miss Thorvaldson. I explained how I'd paid Miss Thorvaldson several lovely compliments and how she'd responded by lashing out at me for no good reason.

"What do you think her problem is?" I asked.

My aunt Maud said she had no idea. "You were sincere when you complimented her, weren't you?" she asked anxiously. When I replied, "Of course — what do you think I am, some kind of nincompoop?" she said that if that were the case, a small gesture emphasizing my genuine fondness for Miss Thorvaldson would probably work wonders.

•••••

I bought Miss Thorvaldson a beautiful card that says "Thinking of You." Inside, I wrote a short note apologizing for any misunderstanding between us. I then attached the card to the giant frozen Thanksgiving turkey my mother bought last week and put the whole thing in an enormous gift box. I am so genuinely fond of turkey that I thought it would be the perfect peace offering — symbolic of my feelings for Miss Thorvaldson and tasty, all at the same time.

Rather than hand her the gift in front of the prying eyes of those baboons I call classmates, I had the school secretary, Trish, deliver it to her in the staff room. I feel certain that this will fix things between her and me.

•••••

Miss Thorvaldson has called a meeting with my parents concerning what she calls my "inappropriate behavior." I can't imagine what she's referring to. The last time I checked, there was no law against giving gifts to teachers, and if she's talking about my flatulence, well, that's a medical condition I have no control over. It might have something to do with the fact that the school secretary, Trish, told Miss Thorvaldson that I'm always staring at her breasts, though I've already done my best to clear up that misunderstanding. It's not that I stare at Trish's breasts, only that I'm fascinated by the interesting stitching on her breast pockets. To prove it, this afternoon I even said to Miss Thorvaldson, "I didn't notice. Does Trish have breasts?" In response, she gave me another detention.

I'm starting to feel very defeated by Miss Thorvaldson's attitude. She isn't trying to meet me halfway at all.

• • • • •

Because of Miss Thorvaldson, I have to start seeing the school psychologist once a week in order to discuss my socially inappropriate behavior! I am mortified. What if I say the wrong thing? I could spend the rest of my life in a wretched institution.

My father thinks I'm overreacting, my mother thinks I should buy her a new turkey with my paper route money and John Michael thinks I shouldn't reveal any of my dark secrets to the psychologist, because he once saw a movie where the psychologist turned out to be the hideous villain's evil henchman.

We'll see about that, but it goes without saying that I'm no longer interested in improving my relationship with Miss Thorvaldson. I'm certain she lies awake at night dreaming up reasons to dislike me.

• • • • •

I'm still in hot water with Lyle Filbender. I've been avoiding him, but today he flung an eraser at my head and whispered, "Pencil dick!" so I reported him to Miss Thorvaldson, who ordered him to apologize. I was as magnanimous as could be when he came groveling to me like the little worm that he is. Nevertheless, I could tell he was bent out of shape over the experience, because later, when I said, "What do you expect when you call people 'pencil dick'?" he punched his fist into a locker and stomped away.

I can't believe I'm the one seeing a psychologist while they let someone like Lyle Filbender roam the halls free. Our system is definitely flawed.

• • • • •

My psychologist has turned out to be a fine-looking woman named Dr. Anderson. During our first session, she offered me Kraft caramels and laughed at a few of my jokes. It is hard to believe that she is Miss Thorvaldson's evil henchman.

• • • • •

We had John Michael and his family over for dinner this weekend. It was a lovely affair. The roast my mother prepared was a little dry and the potatoes could have used more butter, but Mrs. Sweetgrass brought an entire tray of cream puff pastries, along with several home-made pies and a heaping bowl of whipped cream. I was so overwhelmed by the sight of it all that I actually got misty-eyed. John Michael's little sister, Lucy, noticed and asked if I was crying because I had a boo-boo.

I ignored her, of course. A three year old can hardly be expected to understand the complexity of my inner landscape.

• • • • •

Mr. Fitzgerald, my boss at the *Winnipeg Daily News*, called this afternoon to ask if I've been dumping my next-door neighbor's paper onto the boulevard in front of his house. I confessed that I'm often too winded to make it all the way to Mr. Miller's front door and pointed out that any reasonable, able-bodied man should have no problem retrieving his paper from wherever it happened to fall out of my bag. "However, in the spirit of compromise," I added, "if Mr. Miller could henceforth see his way clear to meeting me halfway, I would certainly be willing to do the same."

Mr. Fitzgerald wheezed into the phone for a moment, then snarled, "I'm not interested in compromise, kid. Your job is to deliver the paper to the door. Am I clear?"

I exhaled loudly in order to convey what a bore I thought he was being, then replied, "Fine. Whatever."

Not interested in compromise? What kind of attitude is that? I have decided that Mr. Fitzgerald is a very poor role model for children my age.

●●●●●

I almost got out of delivering papers this morning. I had it all planned out. When my mother came in to wake me, I simply lay there like an unconscious person. After a few minutes of calling my name and jostling me, she gave up and left the room. Pleasantly surprised by her gullibility, I nestled deeper under my cozy *Star Wars* comforter and was just drifting back to sleep when she burst into the room, hit the lights and threw a soaking facecloth on my head. I gasped for air — I felt sure I was having a heart attack! — and my mother cried, "Thank goodness you're alive!" After I recovered, I testily suggested that in the future, she start by checking my pulse.

"What a good idea," she replied, yanking the comforter off the bed. "Now up you get."

Despite this rude awakening, I delivered all my papers — even Mr. Miller's. While it is true that I didn't technically deliver it to his mailbox, I figured that flinging it in the general direction of his front door was close enough, unless he's the kind of person who likes to make problems. Some people live to make life difficult for others, you know.

• • • • •

My grandmother called this evening to upbraid my father for failing to get the inventory of lavender toilets down to a manageable level after almost six weeks on the job. When he protested that overall inventory levels were down by almost sixteen percent already, she said it wouldn't be much comfort when he landed us all in the poorhouse for want of a little attention to lavender toilets. After my father hung up in exasperation, I called my grandmother back and thanked her for having the courage to say what needed to be said. She replied that I was the apple of her eye and wondered why some people couldn't see that she was only trying to help.

• • • • •

Felix from the pawnshop and Marv from the gas station came by the House of Toilets to ask my father to join their organization — Business in Support of Business. Most of the store managers in the area belong to BISOB, the aim of which is to improve the local business climate, either through hands-on community improvement projects or by lobbying the municipal government for favorable treatment. My father is thrilled — even more thrilled than when he was invited to join the Brotherhood of Produce Professionals back in his FoodBarn days. He says he's really starting to believe he can make it at the House of Toilets.

I'm reserving judgment until I see how he handles those lavender toilets.

•••••

This morning at the Mission, Jerry had me working in the food depot putting together food kits for the people who are eligible to come by and pick up free groceries every two weeks. The basic kit contains a dried noodle product, a canned noodle product, a can of soup and a can of fruit or vegetables. I examined a number of these kits and was shocked to discover that some people had lima beans or artichoke hearts for their vegetable.

"What kind of people eat lima beans and artichoke hearts?" I asked.

"The kind of people who have no choice," Jerry replied. When I said I wouldn't eat lima beans unless someone held my feet to hot coals, he said, "You have no idea what you'd eat if you were hungry enough."

At that point, I could tell that he was about to launch into another one of his rambling speeches about the hardships of poverty, so I tried to change the subject by asking if he belonged to BISOB. He said that he didn't, and also that the organization was a thorn in his side because they seemed to feel that poverty was bad for business.

Again with the poverty! I tell you, the guy's obsessed.

•••••

I've had my second session with Dr. Anderson and I think things are going well. When I confided that I

wouldn't be able to reveal too many of my dark secrets to her because she's Miss Thorvaldson's evil henchman, she seemed to be okay with it, and at the end of the session, when I complimented her on her fine approach to psychology, she looked pleased. I guess even intelligent women are susceptible to flattery.

On the other hand, I've had several Family Life classes and so far they've been a big disappointment. Mr. Bennet, our teacher, keeps saying that there's a lot more to think about than penis-in-vagina. The first time he said this, I shouted, "I couldn't agree more!" Then I realized he was talking about emotional preparedness, not foreplay. What a yawn! I privately expressed to Mr. Bennet my concern that the other students were getting bored with all his yammering about respecting yourself and others, and suggested that a brief instructional video might be just the thing to spice up the class, but he laughed and replied, "There'll be plenty of time for all that."

Easy for him to say! He's a swarthy, muscular specimen who's probably had many sexual encounters. I, on the other hand, am a relative novice, and would appreciate a little guidance, if that's not too much to ask from the public school system. Honestly! Sometimes I don't know why we pay taxes.

●●●●●

Things are finally heating up in Family Life class. Today, the boys got to see a video called *Becoming a Man*. The narrator was an ugly chap named Randy who wore a maroon turtleneck and plaid pants. He talked about masturbation and wet dreams, and I tried to look interested, but not too interested, and definitely not so interested that someone might think that these things applied to me. Randy also talked about having uncontrollable erections, and I am very nervous about this. I would be humiliated if I got an erection in front of Mrs. Sweetgrass, and if it happened in front of Dr. Anderson she would probably classify me as a sexual deviant. I hope my excessive worrying doesn't render me impotent, another subject that Randy touched upon.

While we boys were watching our film, the girls were in another room watching one called *It's Wonderful Being a Woman*. Afterward, I grinned and asked Missy Shoemaker if the film had lots of excellent booby shots. When, in a loud voice, she replied, "NO, IT WAS MOSTLY ABOUT MENSTRUATION" I clapped my hands over my ears and fled the classroom to avoid hearing more.

Hang on a second ... NO, I DID NOT JUST SHOUT OUT THE WORD MENSTRUATION, MOM. I SAID "MEN'S STATION." IT'S A NEW HARD ROCK RADIO STATION THAT ALL THE GUYS ARE LISTENING TO THESE DAYS ... WHAT? ... NO, I DON'T KNOW WHETHER IT'S AM OR FM ... I DON'T KNOW IF THE D.J.'S NAME IS K.O. TEX ... OH, WAIT I GET IT — KOTEX! VERY FUNNY, MOM. WOULD YOU JUST LEAVE ME ALONE, PLEASE?

God, talking to her is so embarrassing sometimes!

● ● ● ● ●

I've decided that Jerry's street people have some pretty short memories. I'm still serving them soup every week and they don't treat me at all like a hero. Last Saturday, a guy in workboots and a lumber jacket was giving me a hard time because I wouldn't give him an extra bun. When I reminded him that I was the youth who had handed out free money a while back, he just muttered, "What have you done for me lately?" and made another swipe at the buns.

Later, I complained to Jerry that people like that were exactly why I didn't have extra buns to throw around. "Maybe if they'd show a little more gratitude," I griped, "someone would see fit to donate a few more buns."

Jerry said the poor shouldn't have to prostrate themselves with gratitude in order to eat and reminded me that everyone was entitled to a little personal dignity. I said a full stomach was more important than personal dignity, but Jerry said he wasn't so sure.

•••••

John Michael's friend Daryl Flick wants us to hang out Friday night. John Michael has told me all about this Daryl Flick character. He wears his hair in a long black ponytail and his cousin belongs to a gang. I find this fascinating, because at our school we don't have any gangs at all, unless you want to play Butch Cassidy with the grade 3 kids who'll only let an older kid play if he promises to be the dim-witted big brother of one of the eight-year-old hotshots. As you can imagine, this doesn't command nearly as much respect as hanging out with the relative of a vicious gang member. I only hope Daryl Flick will not be successful in luring me into his cousin's illegal activities. I'm certain that my psychologist, Dr. Anderson, would be disappointed in me if I were involved in a heist.

•••••

As planned, I hung out with Daryl Flick and John

Michael last night. Daryl Flick was exactly as I pictured him — uncouth and uncivilized with an acid tongue that he used on me several times when I tried to throw my arm across his shoulders in a show of camaraderie. We spent several hours standing around outside 7-Eleven being belligerent to store patrons, and it goes without saying that we looked extremely cool, which is probably why three high school foxes in tight jeans decided to linger nearby. In my most suave voice, I commended them for not looking down upon the lads and me because we were only thirteen. Then I sidled closer to the skinny blonde with the goopy eye makeup and murmured, "I've always had a yen for older women." After the ladies hurried away, Daryl called me a big doink. When I explained that name-calling hurt my feelings, he called me a big, fat doink, so I said, "Same to you!" and he seized my terrycloth headband and flung it into the garbage bin.

Later, we went back to Daryl's house, though I didn't stay for long because there was nowhere to sit. "Why don't you sit there?" asked Daryl, gesturing toward a stained old couch covered with cracker crumbs. I pointed to the dirty underwear poking up between two lumpy cushions and explained that I was unusually fastidious where other people's soiled laundry was concerned. "Oh," said Daryl. "I understand completely." Then he waited until my back was turned to drag me to the ground and pull the filthy underpants over my head.

I suspect that if I continue to hang out with Daryl, I will turn into a hooligan myself. Already I'm developing an attitude — for instance, when I got home and my mother asked if I'd had fun, I gave her a scornful

look and stomped upstairs. Later, I came down for cookies and warm milk, but I think she got my initial message loud and clear.

•••••

It was raining hard this morning, and I accidentally dropped several newspapers into a giant mud puddle when I tried to leap over it in order to save myself the bother of walking around it. Unfortunately, Mr. Miller ended up with one of the muddy newspapers because he's last on my route. I think his was also missing the entertainment section, because when I dropped the papers, one of those blew into the road and got run over by a car. I considered going after it, but it looked pretty mangled. Besides, I could've been struck by oncoming traffic during the retrieval operation, and I think I can safely say that none of us would have wanted me to take that risk.

•••••

Mr. Fitzgerald says that if he gets one more complaint about me, I'm in big trouble. Apparently, his star carrier is a girl my age who's looking for a third route anyway. I'm sure he was talking about Missy Shoemaker. Three paper routes! It is these kinds of girls who try to make boys look bad that make girls look bad. Ask anyone.

•••••

My paper route continues and the weather is getting colder. Halloween is right around the corner, and after that it'll be snowing. I can't take much more of this. I only earn about twenty dollars a week before tips, and my tips have been pretty poor.

Perhaps Mr. Miller has been spreading rumors about me.

• • • • •

Tonight after dinner, Ruth dropped by to see if I wanted to do a walkathon for Single Moms Caught in the Welfare Trap. I asked if she would once again be buying me all the Mr. Juicy hot dogs I could eat.

"Your hot dogs cost me thirty dollars at the last rally," she complained. "Don't you think that money would be more appropriately donated to the cause?"

"Not really," I said, adding that if hot dogs were off the table, I'd take a pass. When she expressed disappointment, I said, "What do you expect when my reward for donating money to Jerry's street people is four months of forced servitude in his crummy soup kitchen?" I explained that the whole experience had really put a sour taste in my mouth when it came to getting involved in other people's problems.

"But good luck with it," I called after her, as she stomped off in search of my mother. "Say hello to Mr. Juicy for me."

• • • • •

I met two of the exotic dancers from the Montgomery Hotel and Lounge this morning when I stopped in at the Blue Moon Café before doing my paper route. I learned that they were exotic dancers while eavesdropping on their conversation. After that, I couldn't stop ogling them. They pretended not to notice me at first, but then I introduced myself as a fashion journalist from *Vogue* magazine in Paris, and they were all over me. They asked things like "Do you know Ralph Lauren?"

and "When do you think gauchos will make a come-back?" I answered all their questions and then, in order to seem extra continental, I leaned over and gave each a kiss on the hand.

This turned out to be a fatal error, however, because the dancers were sitting near the door and just as I leaned over, it opened suddenly, sending me flying head-first into a table. I was so stunned that I just lay where I'd fallen, waiting for someone to call 911. When no one did, I leaped to my feet in order to berate them all for their unfeeling attitudes and hit my head on the table again, knocking myself nearly unconscious.

By this time, the dancers — Honey and Penny — were laughing much harder than I thought necessary, and even Mrs. Sweetgrass was smiling, though she did have the courtesy to ask me if I was okay. Then I recognized the reckless door opener — it was Mr. Miller! He didn't even apologize, either. He just said, "Next time, watch where you're standing," and told me his paper better be on time today.

I don't think I'll be patronizing the Blue Moon Café again anytime soon. I've been humiliated in front of those women! I'm not normally a vengeful fellow, but I've decided that I'm going to get Mr. Miller for this. A man has to defend his honor, you know.

●●●●●

I spoke with John Michael and Daryl Flick, and they said that the best time to get Mr. Miller would be Halloween night.

"People expect guys like us to do a little damage on Halloween," explained Daryl. "It's tradition!" When I asked if our prank might include slanderous attacks on Mr. Miller's character, Daryl said, "Yes, and also maybe dog poop in his mailbox."

And people say that the youth of today have no sense of tradition.

• • • • •

There's going to be a Halloween dance at school. Miss Thorvaldson and Mr. Bennet are going to chaperone, and they're sending home a letter to invite any parents who'd like to attend. It goes without saying that I'm going to intercept the letter and tear it into a million tiny pieces before setting it on fire. Attending my first dance is exactly the kind of thing my parents would do, because it is their mission in life to embarrass me by alerting the world to their existence.

Luckily, the dance isn't on Halloween night, so it won't interfere with our plans for Mr. Miller. He remains in my bad books. Yesterday morning, on the way to pick up my papers, I bumped into Honey and Penny. Honey asked, "Are you going on another trip anytime soon?" I didn't understand what she was talking about until Penny pretended to trip and go flying into a table and they both started laughing. I chuckled, too, because I didn't want to seem like a bad sport, but inside I was a seething volcano. It is obvious that those women no longer take me seriously, and it is all Mr. Miller's fault.

• • • • •

My parents have decided to attend the Halloween dance. I was shocked when they gave me the bad news. As planned, I'd destroyed the letter, but apparently Miss Thorvaldson called to personally invite them. I should have known! With the help of my fine-looking psychologist, I'm doing my best to work through my negative feelings for Miss Thorvaldson; it is obvious, however, that she is not putting the same effort into working through her negative feelings for me.

Naturally, I pleaded with my parents to stay away from the dance. My mother refused, saying that she and my father loved supporting my extracurricular activities.

"A lot of kids your age would appreciate having parents who cared enough to get involved," she added. When I said, "Name one," she marched me to my room on account of rudeness.

I really think my mother has to learn the difference between rudeness and honesty.

•••••

Janine Schultz stopped by my desk in Language Arts today to ask if I was going to the dance. I said, "Who wants to know?" Then I didn't know what to say, so I ignored her until she left. I was feeling pretty good about how I'd handled the situation until Missy Shoemaker did a cross-eyed, drooling impression of lovesick me. Apparently, Lyle Filbender thought this was pretty funny, because he laughed like a hyena until I called him a revolting pizza face, at which point he grabbed my best velour shirt and jostled me so violently that I had no choice but to report him to Miss Thorvaldson.

Later, I told Missy Shoemaker that she'd looked highly unattractive when she was doing her impression of me and that no guy was going to look at her twice if she didn't learn to control herself in situations like that. She wiggled her baby finger at me in the universal gesture for a flaccid, extra-small penis, hit the sewing machine pedal and very nearly succeeded in stitching my hand to her Home Economics project.

She is by far the worst girl I know. She must be a major disappointment to her parents.

• • • • •

I'm going to dress up as a doctor for Halloween. In addition to lending me an old stethoscope and lab coat, my mother has persuaded my father to temporarily part with his beloved bowling bag in order to equip me with a proper-looking medical bag.

I tell you, I look so good that if I weren't already destined to become a wealthy playboy, I might actually consider becoming a healer.

• • • • •

Tomorrow is the school dance, and I've been practicing my moves in front of the mirror because it's important that I make a good impression. A person's first dance pretty much sets the tone from then on.

• • • • •

I'm not speaking to my parents because they showed up to my school dance dressed as Fred Astaire and Ginger Rogers, whoever they are. I tried to flee the building the minute they started waltzing around the gymnasium, but Miss Thorvaldson had already interrupted the music and introduced them over the loudspeaker as my parents, so there was no escape. After they finished embarrassing me by dancing together, they walked around, chatting and joking with my friends and teachers, which was even worse.

At the end of the evening, Missy Shoemaker, who was dressed like a Winnipeg Blue Bomber football player, smacked me on the back and declared my parents a hoot, Lyle Filbender declared them fruitcakes and Miss Thorvaldson promised to invite them to every school function from now until the end of time.

My life is ruined.

• • • • •

My mother just asked why I'm so upset and I told her, "If you don't know, we're in bigger trouble than I thought."

That ought to keep her on her toes.

• • • • •

This evening, as he was tucking me into bed, my father asked if I was upset because he'd told that young lady in the football uniform that he hoped I'd be lucky enough to marry a nice, bright girl like her someday.

As I said — ruined!

• • • • •

This afternoon, while we were studying "Our Solar System" in Science class, Missy Shoemaker whispered that she wouldn't marry me if I were the last man on Earth. I pointed out that if I were the last man on Earth, I wouldn't bother getting married because every female alive would want a piece of me. I said I'd start with the ones that had the biggest boobs and work my way down, so she could expect a call in about a hundred million light-years. She rolled her eyes and said, "Light-years are a measurement of distance, not time, you bonehead," but I could tell I'd hit a nerve.

• • • • •

I wore my Halloween costume to the Holy Light Mission this morning. While I was dishing out soup, a scrawny old lady with a twitchy eye called me "Doctor" and asked if I'd check out her arm. Before I could bark at her to move it along, she thrust a pus-covered scab in my face and whined, "I've been picking it for days and it smells funny!" I recoiled in horror and ran to hide among the kitchen women, but Jerry found me and dragged me out front again. Then he gently led the twitchy-eyed lady to the first-aid station, where he applied antiseptic and a clean dressing before offering to drive her to a walk-in clinic if she felt up to it.

When I got home, I told my mother that my work at the Mission was taking a terrible toll and that if I didn't get out of there soon, it could adversely impact my ability to single-handedly repopulate the Earth someday.

Typically, she didn't take my concern seriously. And she wonders why I get upset.

•••••

Tonight is Halloween and I've spent the day collecting dog poop to put in Mr. Miller's mailbox. When I asked Daryl why I had to collect the poop, he said, "There was a vote. You were elected."

I must have missed that meeting.

•••••

My Halloween revenge on Mr. Miller did not go as smoothly as planned, which is too bad because the evening started on a real high note when Lyle Filbender leaped out of some bushes and attacked me. I wouldn't normally consider this a high note, except that he immediately got a dose of his own medicine in the form of John Michael kicking his legs out from under him and pinning him to the sidewalk. I applauded loudly, and when Lyle started to scream that he was going to kill me, I told him, "Stop exaggerating." Then I slapped him in the face with my stethoscope until I felt the joke had gone far enough, at which point I jogged to the end of the block and hollered at John Michael to release the sniveling invertebrate.

Who would have thought that after being humiliated in this way, Lyle Filbender would hunt me down and *actually* try to kill me? Not me, obviously. But that is exactly what happened a few hours later, when John Michael, Daryl Flick and I were busy quietly defiling Mr. Miller's personal property. John Michael — who was dressed up as Dolly Parton — had just crouched down beside me to scrawl insults on Mr. Miller's sidewalk, when, from out of nowhere, Lyle Filbender charged.

Everything was kind of a blur after that. I remember the awkward, terrified scramble to my feet; I remember shouting for help and running to and fro as Lyle Filbender advanced upon me, and Dolly Parton advanced upon him. Then I remember noticing the graceful swell of Dolly's cleavage, and the next thing I knew, a big rock went sailing past my head and crashed through Mr. Miller's front window.

After that, we scattered in all directions. A porch light went on across the street, and an old lady came out to see what was going on, but by then, there was nothing to see, so she went back inside. I hid behind a bush for a few more minutes, then slipped into my house, shoved my costume under my bed and told my parents that I'd been home for hours in order to establish an alibi for myself.

•••••

Mr. Miller came around today asking if anyone had information about his broken window. I said no, and tried to make my face as blank as possible. After he left I called him "Good Old Mr. Miller" to show my parents I had no hard feelings toward the man.

As you can see, I'm building a solid defense around myself. I guess I would make an expert criminal.

● ● ● ● ●

Daryl Flick called today and boy, was he mad. He said I acted like a big dork the other night and that I could have gotten us into real trouble. When I said, "I have absolutely no idea what you're talking about," he pointed out that we were in the middle of vandalizing someone's property when I started shouting for help as loudly as I could and running in circles like some kind of idiot.

"And what's wrong with your arms, anyway?" he asked. "Why do they flap around like that when you run?"

I explained that I'd been utilizing my patented flailing motion in order to gain the momentum needed to hurl myself at Lyle Filbender and rip him to pieces with my bare hands.

"Sure," said Daryl. "And I've got three left nuts."

Lucky!

● ● ● ● ●

I've finally discovered the source of the putrid odor that's been befouling my room these last four days. It had been a real mystery until last night, when my father mentioned that his senior men's bowling league was starting up and I suddenly remembered that in my panic

on Halloween night, I'd flung his bowling bag under my bed still stuffed with the dog poop and rotten eggs we'd planned to load into Mr. Miller's mailbox.

I've managed to remove the larger chunks of shell and excrement with one of my mother's spatulas, but I don't know how I'm going to get rid of the smears and the stench. Maybe I'll try her nail file and half a bottle of her Chanel perfume. We'll see. The only thing I know for sure at this point is that there's no use trying to purchase a replacement bag. This one is made of genuine leather and has the words "Pride of Saskatchewan" stitched in fancy gold letters across the side. Bowling bags like that don't grow on trees, you know.

•••••

Lyle Filbender hasn't said a word to me at school, but if this is his way of trying to be nice so I won't tell on him, he's got another thing coming. I've decided to sing like a canary if they catch me. I would only crack under questioning, anyway.

•••••

This evening at dinner, the doorbell rang. It was Mr. Miller again, this time with some photos that the lady across the street took through her bay window on Halloween night. Apparently, she'd been expecting young punks to get up to no good that particular evening, and so, in her capacity as a member of the Neighborhood Watch, she'd sat in the dark with her camera like some kind of lunatic, waiting to catch them in the act.

Unfortunately, the old bat got a perfect shot of Dolly Parton trying to disarm Lyle Filbender as he attempted to strangle me with my own stethoscope. I was fully prepared to play the role of the falsely accused innocent party until I noticed the demonic look on my mother's face and decided that the safer course of action would be to make a quick confession in the hopes that I'd score points for honesty. I owned up to everything, though I stressed that John Michael, Daryl Flick and I had only intended to pull some innocent, boyish pranks and that Lyle Filbender had been the one with the truly evil intentions. I shook my head gravely and said, "We're lucky he hit the window and not his real target — my head — because otherwise, we could have been talking murder!" I waited for my parents to break down sobbing at the thought of their only child dead, but they didn't even sniffle, so I hurried on to point out that in addition to trying to kill me, Lyle Filbender had flung a large portion of my Halloween treats on the sidewalk earlier in the evening.

"So you see, in a way, some of my personal property was destroyed, as well," I said. "Isn't that punishment enough?"

I thought it was an excellent point, but the large vein on my mother's forehead had begun to throb, so I let it drop.

If there's one thing I know, it's when to back off.

$$\bullet \ \bullet \ \bullet \ \bullet \ \bullet$$

My parents met with the parents of my accomplices, and Daryl Flick and Lyle Filbender ended up getting off. Can you believe it? What's more shocking is that Lyle Filbender's parents are upstanding citizens. His father — a podiatrist — has an office in the neighborhood strip mall and belongs to BISOB, and his mother is a good old-fashioned housewife. She even brought fresh-baked chocolate-chip cookies to the punishment conference! Ironically, I think my mother could take a few tips from Mrs. Filbender, though I haven't bothered to mention this to her. She rarely responds well to constructive criticism.

Anyway, Lyle swore that it couldn't be him in the photograph, because he'd been playing pinball with Daryl when the picture was taken. Daryl confirmed his alibi, conveniently providing an alibi for himself in the process. Since Lyle's parents seemed satisfied with this laughable explanation and Daryl's mother hadn't shown up, the whole thing ended up getting pinned on John Michael and me. Now we have to clean out Mr. Miller's basement for him and we're both grounded for three weeks except for work and volunteer commitments. The only sliver of light in the darkness is that our parents agreed to split the cost of the deductible to have the window replaced instead of heaping this burden upon us as well.

On my way to bed, I thanked my parents for showing me this minuscule mercy and complimented them for graciously accepting the price of their inadequate parenting. My mother snapped that I was lucky they didn't believe in corporal punishment or else she would have paddled me black and blue. I commended her on her policy of not being physically abusive toward me but pointed out that even the threat of physical violence can scar a child emotionally. Then I asked, "Are you planning to bring me warm milk in bed?" She said that she was not.

Oh, well. I tried.

•••••

John Michael and I cleaned out Mr. Miller's basement this afternoon. It was disgusting. The sewer had backed up last spring and he hadn't been downstairs since. I took one look at the place and marched back home to put on full sanitary gear, including a face mask, gown and latex gloves from my mother's public health nurse cache. Mr. Miller seemed offended when I reentered his home looking like a scientist from a biohazard facility, but I wasn't willing to be infected with some vile disease just to protect his delicate sensibilities.

Needless to say, we worked like slaves and Mr. Miller didn't offer us any refreshments. In fact, when I suggested that he pay a visit to God's Grocery Store and pick up a few cartons of the Milk of Human Kindness, he just glared and ordered me out of his bathroom.

Mr. Miller must have many unresolved issues. There is clearly something eating him up inside.

●●●●●

I have had television privileges taken away for a week because my father discovered the rotten eggs and dog excrement caked inside his Pride of Saskatchewan bowling bag. He was so upset that he couldn't stop retching. I sensed that things were about to go badly for me again, so I quickly confessed that I'd seen Lyle Filbender following stray dogs around the park with a garden spade and apologized for allowing him to slip poop into my medical bag when I wasn't looking. Unfortunately, my mother didn't buy it for a minute. She said that what I'd done was wrong and gross and that the greater transgression was that I'd lied about it. I gave her a nasty look and said, "I wasn't talking to you" and that's when she snatched away my television privileges.

I think my mother should learn to butt out when people aren't talking to her. Perhaps I'll mention this to her, if I can find the right way to phrase it. As you can tell, she often gets bent out of shape over semantics.

• • • • •

While we were standing around the hall at school today, Missy Shoemaker told me that Mr. Fitzgerald told her that Mr. Miller requested a new paper delivery person. She said she'd heard all about my asinine little stunt on Halloween.

"Are you ever planning to grow up?" she asked.

"I don't know," I replied. "Are you ever planning to grow some boobs?"

She called me an ignoramus, so I called her the President of the Itty Bitty Titty Committee. Then she laughed and told me to get some new material, so I flung my eraser and it hit her underdeveloped left breast.

Well, you'd think that I'd poked her eye out! She threw up her hands, let out a big cry and charged into the classroom. The next thing I knew, I was standing at attention listening to Miss Thorvaldson give me a long, boring speech about respecting each other's bodies. When she was finished, I explained how Missy Shoemaker had implied that I was unimaginative and suggested that she give Missy a speech about respecting each other's feelings, and I got a detention.

Later, I was tempted to make another snide remark to Missy Shoemaker about her lack of cleavage, but I resisted. Miss Thorvaldson obviously has a soft spot where Missy Shoemaker and her budding breasts are concerned. Why else would she have overreacted that way?

•••••

I called Mr. Fitzgerald to find out if what Missy Shoemaker said about Mr. Miller wanting a new paper delivery person was true, and Mr. Fitzgerald confirmed that it was. "I heard all about your little stunt, too, kid," he grunted. "So you can just consider yourself on probation."

Probation! Needless to say, I was shocked. I asked Mr. Fitzgerald by what process my probation status had been determined. When he replied, "By the process of my saying so," I told him it didn't sound like a very objective method to me. I pointed out that it almost sounded undemocratic, though I softened the comment by adding, "I'm sure you didn't mean to sound like a fascist dictator." I don't think he was very softened, though, because he sounded rather grouchy when he hung up.

The upshot is that I'm going to be very chilly toward Mr. Miller from now on, since I consider it his fault that I'm on probation. There was no good reason to request a new paper delivery person — his smashed window had nothing to do with the delivery of his paper, and I have been giving him top customer service for several days now. It is obvious that he called Mr. Fitzgerald just to be spiteful, and I can't stand people who hold a grudge.

Tape #2

I asked the second Wise Man to
spit on the Virgin Mary during our
next rehearsal as a personal favor
to me, but he refused.
And I thought we were friends.

The members of BISOB held a community improvement rally tonight. Their goal was to clean up the empty lot next door to the Holy Light Mission. That lot is a real burr under Marv's saddle because it's right across the street from his gas station, and he thinks the sight of all that garbage and graffiti drives off paying customers. Plus, it's a big hangout for the squeegee kids who stand on the boulevard washing the windshields of cars stopped for red lights.

"What have you got against clean windshields, Marv?" I asked, as we tossed discarded pop cans into the recycling bin.

"Those kids are a nuisance the way they try to guilt decent folks into coughing up a dollar," he griped. When I said that a dollar sounded like a fair price to pay for a sparkling windshield, he glared at me and went to help Mr. Filbender haul away a burned mattress, so I grabbed two more free hot dogs from Mr. Juicy and wandered off to tell my father about my conversation with Marv.

"You'd better hope BISOB doesn't hear about that spare change tin you keep in the car," I whispered. My father agreed that it might reflect poorly on his status as a BISOB member to be seen supporting the squeegee kids and asked if I'd take over his change dispensing duties. I told him to forget it.

"It's not my problem that you don't have the courage of your convictions," I said. Then I asked for some money because the Dickie Dee ice-cream man had just pulled up and his Itsakadoodle Pops are the cat's meow.

My father gave me a sour look and muttered, "I don't think I can spare the change."

Can you believe it? Plenty of change for cold, hungry strangers, no change for an Itsakadoodle Pop for his own flesh and blood. I really think my father needs to get his priorities straight.

• • • • •

This morning before school, my grandmother called with her first lukewarm words of encouragement for my father. She said that Mr. Filbender called to tell her about the rally and that she was pleased to see my father finally getting his priorities straight. I'd been quietly listening in on the cordless phone since the beginning of the call, and when she said this, I shouted, "Are you kidding me?" and tried to explain how he'd denied me an Itsakadoodle Pop. Unfortunately, my mother barged into my room without warning and wrestled the phone away from me before I could finish my explanation. I was about to berate her for not respecting my privacy, when she suddenly noticed the threadbare state of my gitch and asked how long it had been since I'd changed my underwear. This got me very flustered — since I couldn't actually remember — and she was able to give me a short, intrusive speech on the importance of personal hygiene and leave the room before I could come up with a suitably scathing retort.

Just for that, I may never change my underwear again.

• • • • •

This morning when I went to the soup kitchen, I asked Jerry what he thought of Thursday night's BISOB rally. He said that cleaning up the community was always a positive thing, but that he was distressed by the way BISOB members blamed the Mission for the state of the empty lot.

"The Mission doesn't own the property," he pointed out. "And a lot of the people who throw garbage there aren't involved with us in any way." When I murmured, "Tell me more," and settled deeper into my attitude of repose, he told me to quit stalling and get back to work. I said, "That hurts," and also, "The spirit needs nourishment too, you know," but he had already walked away.

Near the end of my shift in the food depot, Honey — one of the exotic dancers from the Montgomery — came in to pick up a single-parent family food kit, some baby formula and diapers. After packing her handouts into the back of a wobbly stroller, she introduced me to her daughter, Bella. Little Bella obviously sensed that I don't have much use for babies, because when I leaned over to give her a bored tickle under the chin, she seized my hair and started yanking with all her might. For some reason, the other mothers in line seemed to find the sight of me writhing in pain very hilarious, and it was some time before they managed to stop laughing for long enough to loosen Bella's death grip on my head.

The minute order was restored, I ran and told Jerry all about the incident. I expressed amazement that Bella had been able to hang on so tightly with all that Dippity-do styling gel in my hair and wondered if I should knock off early on account of the pounding headache that ungrateful baby had given me. Jerry checked my scalp for bald patches, said, "I think you'll live" and told me to take out the garbage before returning to my post.

Talk about ungrateful.

●●●●●

I mentioned to Ruth about how Honey makes ends meet by taking off her clothes in front of perverted strangers at night and collecting life's necessities from the Mission on the weekend.

"Don't you think this woman is a shining example of

how uneducated single mothers can avoid complete dependency on our bleeding-heart social welfare system if they really put their minds to it?" I asked. Ruth told me to get real.

"The only thing that woman is an example of," she said, "is how limited some people's options really are."

I wonder if Ruth's cup is ever half full.

•••••

Mr. Bennet has started a question period in Family Life class during which he answers the embarrassing questions students write down anonymously and stuff surreptitiously into the box at the front of the classroom.

It's an excellent system, but yesterday, Missy Shoemaker broke all the rules. She said that she didn't need to put her question in the box, then came right out and asked what the average length of a man's penis is. My God! I couldn't believe it! She said "penis" in front of Mr. Bennet! Of course, I started giggling — what can you expect when a person says "penis" in mixed company? Missy looked right at me and said, "I wouldn't laugh too hard if I were you, because it probably isn't two inches." This made everyone else laugh. I was extremely offended and looked to Mr. Bennet for support — since I don't think a woman should ever be allowed to insult a person's manhood — but he just answered the question.

"The average length is about five inches erect," he explained. "But don't worry: a little bigger or smaller is still perfectly normal. And besides, in a loving relationship, things like that don't matter." I burst into giggles again, because I couldn't think of any other way to react, but it got me thinking. So I've decided to measure my own unit.

Just a second, I've got to put the tape recorder down. I'm going to need two hands for this ...

... AHHHH! CAN'T YOU EVER KNOCK, MOM? *GOD!* THIS IS SO EMBARRASSING! NEVER MIND WHAT I'M DOING — I'M SCRATCHING, IF YOU REALLY MUST KNOW! YES, I'M USING A RULER TO DO IT. I'M VERY, VERY ITCHY, THAT'S WHY! WHAT? OF COURSE, I'LL BE CAREFUL — I KNOW THEY'RE EXTERNAL ORGANS, MOM! GOD! WOULD YOU JUST GET OUT OF HERE AND LEAVE ME ALONE, PLEASE?

I'm going to have to try this again later. My package has retracted so far up that it's currently nestled somewhere around my tonsils. It'll be hours before I can get an accurate measurement.

$$\bullet \bullet \bullet \bullet \bullet$$

I measured my unit again — this time in the locked bathroom — and to my horror, found that it was only two inches long! How did Missy Shoemaker know? I'm going to check the boys' locker room. Perhaps she drilled a hole in the wall. I wouldn't be surprised — as I've said, she's a very vulgar young woman.

Anyway, given a five-inch average, I'm understandably upset by my discovery. Wouldn't it be ironic if I ended up being deformed in this area, when I'm such an excellent specimen in every other way? Perhaps I should see a specialist.

$$\bullet \bullet \bullet \bullet \bullet$$

Over dinner last night, I announced that I'd like to see a specialist. When my parents asked what kind of specialist, I told them it was a private matter and that they should mind their own business and stop trying to embarrass me.

"Are you sick?" asked my mother with a worried look on her face.

"No," I replied coolly. "But it's possible that I'm suffering from some sort of genetic deformity." At this, I looked straight at my father, hoping they would both get the hint. They didn't get the hint, though, so I said, "Forget it!" and stormed off to my room in a huff.

What if it really is a genetic deformity? I think I'll try for a casual glance at my father getting changed. Perhaps he's passed his inadequacies on to me.

• • • • •

Tonight I burst in on my father getting ready for bed. He was only wearing his striped pajama top and he looked extremely undignified. I find it hard to believe that my mother can take him seriously as a lover. When I become a lover, I will wear black satin pajamas and keep chilled champagne by my bedside at all times.

Anyway, I got a gander at his piece and he looks like he's a little under average, but certainly longer than two inches. I guess my heredity theory is shot. Shoot.

• • • • •

Today in Canadian History we had a substitute teacher. She had fluffy red hair and a knockout figure, and I suddenly found myself overcome by an aching desire to learn more about this great country of ours and also to peek down her shirt. I went to her desk with questions many times, and my efforts were not in vain, because right near the end of class, as she was explaining something about who knows what, her crisp white blouse gaped momentarily and I caught an eyeful of her lacy, off-white brassiere. I gave the guys in the class a discreet double thumbs-up and they made some lewd facial expressions in return, and I was really enjoying my moment in the spotlight when I began to feel some stirring south of the border. While I was somewhat intrigued by this surefire sign of impending puberty, I was mostly just frantic. I told the substitute, "I get it, already!" then snatched my textbook away from her and used it to cover my private region as I sped back to my desk.

My first spontaneous public erection! Wow. I can't recall a more exciting event in Canadian history.

•••••

No specialist in the city would book me without a referral, so this afternoon I went to a walk-in clinic to see a doctor about my two-inch problem. He assured me that I'll probably sprout a "big old kolbassa" once puberty hits. He also said that in the future, I should wait for the physician to ask me to undress instead of taking the initiative. Apparently, the shock of finding a naked little hooligan in his examination room almost stopped his old ticker.

•••••

As I am no longer grounded on account of the Mr. Miller fiasco, my parents have decided to entrust the house to me Saturday night. They say that I'm becoming a young adult and that it's time this was reflected in the kinds of privileges I'm given. I agree wholeheartedly, and have decided to sneak John Michael and Daryl Flick over for the evening. We will watch trashy television, tell tasteless jokes and maybe even order takeout. I can't wait.

•••••

We had a hoot Saturday night and my parents never suspected a thing. I've had a few twinges of guilt at having abused their trust, but these quickly subside when I remind myself that it's all part of growing up.

The lads came by just after my parents left for the evening. We watched *Love Boat* and exchanged filthy comments about Julie, the cruise director, until Daryl brought out some rubbers. There were ribbed, flavored — even glow-in-the-dark! I was trying to imagine what kind of pervert would get up to that kind of kinky business when I realized that the rubber in my hands was slimy. Fearing the worst, I shrieked and flung it across the room. After he stopped laughing, Daryl explained, "It's lubricated, you doorknob, not used," and I couldn't help thinking that these were the kinds of things Mr. Bennet should be filling us in about, not all that stuff about how you can still be a love machine with a two-inch doink.

Anyway, after we opened all the little packages, we rolled some rubbers onto various items from the vegetable crisper and filled others with water from the tap until they burst all over the kitchen floor. Then we had a burping contest, Daryl taught us how to make farting sounds under our armpits and we polished off a bulk box of coconut-frosted Twinkies. The fellows left shortly before my parents arrived back home, and as I watched Daryl urinate against the oak tree in our front yard, all I could think about was what a terrific evening it had been. We are real guys.

• • • • •

My father took me aside today and asked if I'd been rummaging through his night table recently. I said, "Of course not," and wondered why he'd asked. He said that quite a few of his condoms were missing and that he couldn't imagine where they'd gone. Then he looked at me. Then he said, "There's nothing wrong with being curious, son, but taking another guy's condoms without asking is like wearing another guy's jockstrap without asking." At that point, I told him I had to leave the room because I thought I was going to vomit.

Later, over dinner, my mother gave her public health nurse talk about Safe Sex and the importance of using prophylactics to prevent sexually transmitted diseases. She said she was just making conversation, but I sensed that her comments were directed toward me, so I snapped, "I think it's pretty inappropriate to be talking about venereal diseases when we're eating creamed corn, don't you?"

I am mortified. I'm sure that Daryl Flick stole those rubbers from my father's bedside table — it must have been when he left the room to use the bathroom. My God! That means I've played games with my very own parents' prophylactics!

I'm going to kill Daryl Flick for this.

●●●●●

My mother found a rubber under the sofa while she was vacuuming. It must have been the one I flung across the room when I thought it was used, but of course I denied any knowledge of it. Instead, I went on the offensive, shouting, "Don't blame me!" and saying that if she and my father insisted on indulging their sexual perversions, they should at least try not to litter the entire household with the evidence of their fornicating.

In retrospect, perhaps the term "sexual perversion" was a little harsh, but I've been haunted by the image of that glow-in-the-dark prophylactic.

I'm definitely going to kill Daryl Flick for this.

• • • • •

I've acquired my first piece of pornographic material and I am electrified. It is a *Playboy* magazine and it's a loaner from Daryl Flick. He says he's sorry for stealing my parents' rubbers, but I've told him never mind. *Playboy!* Daryl Flick is a great friend. The Playmate of the Month is a stunning brunette named Electra Donovan and she has spectacular breasts. The article says she's studying to become a serious actress and I sure hope she makes it. She would look terrific on the big screen.

My mother wants to know why I've been spending so much time in my room these days and I keep telling her it's because I'm studying.

"I've come to realize that education is a privilege," I explain. "And I just want to make the most of it."

I don't enjoy deceiving her, but I can't tell her the truth, which is that I am looking at pictures of naked women. She would take it entirely out of context.

• • • • •

I had an extra-long session with Dr. Anderson today. I confessed all about the prophylactics and pornographic material and said I was sure that puberty was right around the corner. When she asked how I felt about this, I declared, "It's about time! I've felt like a man for quite a while now and I'm tired of being treated like a child." She asked me to elaborate, but I just smiled at her.

Afterward, I told her that I felt a real bond developing between us and asked if perhaps I should start calling her by her first name, which is Elizabeth. She said, "I don't think that would be appropriate, and one of the things that we're supposed to be discussing in our sessions is the difference between appropriate and inappropriate behavior, right?"

"Say no more!" I replied, giving her a wink.

She obviously feels the growing bond between us as well and is concerned that something inappropriate might take place between us.

● ● ● ● ●

Today at lunch hour I told John Michael about Dr. Anderson's growing feelings of attraction toward me and swore him to secrecy unless he really felt compelled to share the information with the other guys in the class.

"You're dreaming," he said. "I heard her husband is a former Olympian."

"Emphasis on the word 'former,'" I sniffed, before reminding him that nobody likes a has-been.

Later, John Michael came over to my house to study. After shouting hello to my mother, we dumped our stuff in the front hall, grabbed a bag of Orcos and headed up to my room to study *Playboy* from cover to cover. Some of those articles were really terrific! We also enjoyed the letters to the editor, in which men described their most awesome sexual experiences. Neither of us realized that such outrageous things actually happened to ordinary Joes, or that there were so many sets of gorgeous blond triplets in the world. We both agreed that it gives a guy hope.

● ● ● ● ●

My parents have given me fifteen dollars as a reward for how hard I've been studying these days. My mother

hugged me and said, "It's such a relief not to have to nag you to do your homework."

"I couldn't agree more," I replied. "Your nagging has been a trial to us both."

When I wondered aloud how much Lik-M-Aid I could buy with fifteen dollars, however, she promptly vetoed the purchase of candy on the grounds that she'd like me to enter adulthood with at least a few teeth. She stuck to her guns even after I reminded her how much we both disliked her nagging, so eventually I agreed to allow her to drive me to the mall tomorrow after school so I can purchase some kind of nonedible reward item.

I wonder if the newsstand sells lingerie catalogs.

●●●●●

I didn't get lingerie catalogs or anything else at the mall, because I caught a glimpse of Dr. Anderson at the far end of the food court. It was the first time I'd seen her outside school, and I was so excited by the possibility of getting to know her on a more personal level that I waved, shouted her name and walked directly into the corner of a nearby food court table, nearly crushing my testicles with the force of my confident stride. I immediately shrieked in agony and lurched toward the back of the nearest chair to prevent myself from collapsing. The guy sitting in the chair gave me an elbow jab in the ribs and told me to get lost. He looked like an athletic fellow who'd probably had many experiences with mangled balls, so I dangled a little closer and explained in a whisper that I couldn't move just yet because my testicles were throbbing. Unfortunately, this didn't elicit the sympathetic response I'd been hoping for. Instead, he gave me a violent shove backward, propelling me into a passing shopping cart. The cart swung sideways into an old man, knocking him into the counter of Orange Julius. The lady pushing the cart gave me a vicious look — as though I'd purposely propelled myself into her cart! — and the athletic fellow started laughing at me, as did some of the other food court patrons. I ignored them all and sauntered off as casually as I could, given the fact that every step sent searing pain shooting through my groin. I briefly clung to the hope that Dr. Anderson had noticed the incident and was waiting to deliver first aid — perhaps in the form of a therapeutic massage to the afflicted region — but when I reached the spot where I'd last seen her, she was gone.

I'm really disappointed in that athletic fellow. I think guys should always stick together when someone's testicles are on the line. I'll bet women would stick together if someone's ovaries were on the line, especially women belonging to the radical feminist movement. They are very organized about things like that.

• • • • •

This evening, my mother gave me a lecture on the importance of staying hydrated. Apparently, she's noticed that I haven't been drinking my ice water at dinner these last few days. That's because I've been applying ice packs to my dirty underwear to prevent my injured testicles from swelling up, then secretly returning the half-melted cubes to the tray in order to avoid any embarrassing questions. The thought of drinking water chilled with those ice cubes makes me sick, but since I didn't feel that was any of her business, I said, "Don't worry, Mom. I've been drinking plenty of water while I do my homework."

 Tape #2

She looked so pleased. I guess I have a real way with words sometimes.

•••••

Today during Silent Reading, John Michael passed me a note that said Daryl Flick wanted us to hang out with the squeegee kids on Friday night. I wrote back that it sounded like fun but that I'd have to give it some thought. I reminded John Michael that the members of BISOB were my People and that many of them disliked the squeegee kids.

"Would you want to rock the boat if it went against the beliefs of your People?" I scribbled. I also used up several lines complaining of the bitter cold, and wrote an important P.S. in large capital letters: "MY BALLS HAVEN'T FULLY RECOVERED FROM THE MANGLING THEY RECEIVED AT THE MALL. I PROBABLY SHOULDN'T BE STANDING FOR EXTENDED PERIODS OF TIME UNTIL FURTHER NOTICE."

Exhausted but satisfied, I crumpled my note into a tiny ball and tried to toss it to John Michael. Unfortunately, it hit Missy Shoemaker in the neck and fell down her blouse instead. I whispered, "Oops," and tried to explain that it had been an honest mistake, but she didn't believe me, I guess, because she deftly retrieved it and hurled it at my head with all the speed and power that had made her Most Valuable Player on the all-star provincial softball team last year. I cried out as it struck me in the temple, and Miss Thorvaldson — trailing a sleek silk scarf expertly knotted and thrown over one shoulder — pounced like a gigantic bird of prey that could no longer take flight because it was too gigantic and out of shape.

She read my note aloud without showing a spark of sympathy for my poor testicles, then told John Michael and me that she was going to call our parents to let them know what we were up to. When I gently pointed out that what we did after school hours was really none of her business, she said, "Go stand in the corner for an extended period of time."

She is even less sympathetic than I thought.

• • • • •

My parents have forbidden me to hang out with the squeegee kids. My mother said, "Troubled kids can be real trouble, honey," and my father said, "We love you too much to see you get yourself into a situation you can't handle, son."

After they finished harping on me, I secretly called John Michael and we both agreed that our parents are being overly judgmental in the matter of our dear, good friends the squeegee kids. We also agreed that we are old enough to do as we please whether they like it or not and decided to meet at Daryl Flick's tomorrow after school to make plans.

• • • • •

Daryl was thrilled to learn that we'd be sneaking out behind our parents' backs on Friday. He said he was especially proud of me since I usually act like such a big wuss. I thanked him for his kind words, then asked him to please stop dragging me around the room in a headlock because I was beginning to feel faint. He did a few more laps before shouting, "Hurrah!" and letting me go with a shove that sent me headfirst into his smelly old couch.

He is the most exhausting friend I've ever had.

•••••

We went over to Daryl's house again today, this time to make signs for our squeegee evening. Daryl says that it's going to be too cold to actually wash windshields but that signs asking for money usually work just as well. When he showed us his, which said, "SPARE SOME CHANGE?" I told him it was probably the least imaginative sign I'd ever seen. I made one that said, "MY GIRTH IS NOT THE RESULT OF EATING THREE BALANCED MEALS A DAY BUT RATHER THE PAINFUL BLOAT OF STARVATION. PLUS, MY MOTHER NEEDS AN OPERATION OR ELSE SHE WILL DIE. IF YOU DON'T GIVE WHAT I KNOW YOU CAN SPARE, THERE IS A GOOD CHANCE THE FATES WILL TURN ON YOU." It was really well done — I used a deep magenta marker and put curlicues on all my capital letters. Daryl snorted, "That's the stupidest sign I've ever seen." John Michael added that in Canada, we have a public health care system, so my mother's operation would be paid for.

"There's no telling how long it'll take her to recover from her facelift," I replied confidently, adding another curlicue to my sign. "And we're going to have to hire some expensive household help to care for me in the meantime. Let's see your sign, John Michael."

He held it up. It said, "WALK A MILE IN MY SHOES."

Catchy.

•••••

I made $12.45 tonight before Marv chased us off the boulevard, but I suffered two skinned knees, a serious toe injury and numerous emotional snubs in the process, so I'm not entirely sure it was worth it.

The evening started out around seven o'clock. After telling our parents that we were going to the youth drop-in center up the block, John Michael and I met up with Daryl and we all headed for the boulevard with our signs. To my disappointment, there wasn't a squeegee kid in sight, and no wonder. A bitter, biting wind was blowing hard from the north and it had just started to snow. I wouldn't have been able to stand it if I hadn't been nestled snugly in my lawn chair with a blanket over my lap, wearing my father's down-filled ski jacket and sipping hot chocolate from a thermos. Daryl was obviously jealous of my foresight, because he kept jiggling my lawn chair in an attempt to get me to spill cocoa down the front of my father's jacket.

"It's not my fault you didn't even bother to wear mitts," I told him. "And why didn't you wear one of your warmer jackets?"

In response he toppled me right over into the snow and started jumping back and forth over a nearby cement planter in an effort to keep his sneakered feet from freezing. As I was struggling to right my chair, Daryl suddenly froze, gave a low whistle and said, "What a babe!"

Looking into the backseat of the car stopped at the traffic light, I saw that it was my greatest admirer, Janine Schultz, so I pulled off my balaclava and favored her with a slight toss of my chin. Well! Her whole face lit up at the sight of me, and Daryl shot me such a dumbfounded look that my heart just soared. With an uncharacteristic burst of energy, I launched myself at Daryl in order to engage in some good-natured horseplay.

Unfortunately, I failed to notice that my spilled cocoa had, by this point, frozen into a treacherous ice slick, so instead of bounding forward with youthful vigor, I felt both feet go flying out from under me and I dropped like a sack of hammers. John Michael and Daryl immediately erupted into peals of laughter, and when I staggered to my feet I could see Janine and her parents laughing merrily as they drove off.

I was so enraged that I kicked the cement planter as hard as I could, stubbing my toe so badly that I started shrieking in agony. I guess I made quite a scene because shortly after this, Marv came charging out of his gas station with a baseball bat and we all grabbed our stuff and took off across the empty lot beside the Mission.

Back at Daryl's house, we divided the money three ways, even though I'd barely collected anything because I couldn't be bothered getting out of my lawn chair to make it easy for people to reach my tin can. Then I hobbled home as I best I could in my battered condition and crawled up to my room after advising my parents that the volunteers at the youth drop-in center had done only a mediocre job of entertaining me.

If there's one thing I've learned it's that you have to make your lies believable if you want any hope of credibility.

•••••

It was still snowing with a vengeance this morning, making my miserable paper route even more miserable. Would you believe that some people don't even have the consideration to shovel a path for me? One of my Cougar boots got entirely filled with snow, and by the time I got home, my injured foot was so cold that I could barely drag it up the steps behind me.

Later, over breakfast, I tried to explain to my mother

about the unfeeling cretins to whom I deliver papers.

"Maybe your foot wouldn't have gotten so cold if you'd done up your boot laces and worn socks," she said.

"You're missing the point entirely," I replied, holding out my plate for another stack of pancakes. "The point is that the unfeeling cretins didn't shovel a path for me."

Sometimes my mother just doesn't get it.

● ● ● ● ●

Today at school, I noticed that Janine Schultz wasn't fawning over me as much as she usually does, so I made an extra effort to draw attention to myself by being loud and disruptive in class. Unfortunately, Miss Thorvaldson seemed to think that her math lesson was more important than my self-esteem, so she sent me to the office to write lines. Upon completing them, I tracked down Janine and offered a full explanation for my actions last Friday night, telling her that I'd been collecting money for charity and that I'd fallen on purpose in order to drive home the message of how painful life could be for the average squeegee kid.

"And in addition to donating the entire $12.45 I collected on Friday," I confided, "I plan to donate $15 of my own personal money to the Holy Light Mission, where I willingly volunteer on a regular basis."

Janine seemed somewhat intrigued by my explanation and even said that she admired people who cared enough to get involved. Then she asked me to stop blocking the doorway to the girls' washroom because she was going to be late for class.

I think I've managed to preserve Janine's enormous crush on me. What a relief! I don't think I'd feel half as popular if I ceased to be the object of her unrequited love.

●●●●●

I'm very concerned about my injured toe. At first, it just looked like a regular bruise, but now it's turning horrible shades of green and yellow and my toenail is hanging on by a thread. In addition, I've identified a strange, blistering growth that appears to be spreading rapidly. I'm certain that decay has set in. I briefly considered showing it to my mother, but she didn't have a very high-technology approach to reviving me that morning I pretended to be unconscious, and I'm not interested in having my foot hacked off with a dull kitchen knife.

Perhaps I'll hit the walk-in clinic again.

●●●●●

As soon as I arrived at the Mission this morning, I told Jerry I was facing a high-risk amputation due to a ravaging foot infection. I must say, his level of distress was deeply gratifying.

"When did your doctor give you the news?" he cried.

I allowed him to hug me for several minutes before explaining that a formal diagnosis was pending. He seemed less distressed after that, but still quite interested, and even offered to take a look at my foot. I said all right, because although we both agreed he was no expert, we also agreed that he's seen a few weeping wounds in his day.

After careful examination, Jerry informed me that I have a fungal infection known as athlete's foot. A fungal infection! It is much worse than I imagined. He said there is only one medicated powder that might be able to stop the terrible spread of my disease, and added that this kind of thing is often picked up in public changing rooms. I explained that I never use those kinds of facilities because I abhor physical activity of any kind, but he just shrugged, squirted some anti-bacterial soap onto his hands and said, "Well, you were contaminated somewhere."

Doing my best to ignore this heartless comment, I told Jerry that out of consideration for the health and welfare of the general public I was prepared to immediately return home and voluntarily quarantine myself in front of the television.

"The general public will be just fine as long as you don't serve soup with your toes," he replied. I moaned that I was feeling faint and swayed back and forth to indicate my faintness, but he just said, "You know, there are a lot of people who are a lot worse off than you, who have to work a lot harder than you do just to make ends meet." He grabbed a handful of brown paper towels and started drying his hands. "You should look out across the soup line if you want to see a few of those people," he added. "Now back to work."

I wonder if the olden-days church people made the lepers work this hard. If they did, and if I were a leper, I would have made them find their own colony.

● ● ● ● ●

I've asked my mother to purchase a large container of the medicated powder required to kill the growth that is rapidly enveloping my foot. At first, I didn't use the term "athlete's foot" because it didn't sound very medical — or very dignified — but eventually I got around to mentioning it. My mother laughed and said, "What's next, jock itch?" I gave her my best wounded expression,

but she just told me to lighten up. Lighten up! Some bedside manner. She and Jerry obviously went to the same school for Compassion Training.

●●●●●

I put a question in the Family Life box about jock itch and Mr. Bennet read it in front of the entire class. He explained that jock itch is an irritation that boys and men sometimes get if they don't practice good personal hygiene in the pubic area. I think my ears got very red when he said that, mostly because I realized that my own mother had been thinking about my pubic hygiene when she'd joked about jock itch. Why was she thinking about my pubic hygiene? I think she needs a part-time job. She obviously has too much time on her hands.

Mr. Bennet went on to say that there are several sexually transmitted diseases that can also make the groin area itch. I assume he listed all of them, but I'm not entirely sure, because after he mentioned one called "crabs" I couldn't hear anything except the sound of large, vicious crustaceans snapping at my member.

●●●●●

Speaking of part-time jobs, since we arrived in Winnipeg, my mother has been trying without success to land one at a local hospital. She's now considering branching into less traditional roles for health care professionals. When I suggested that she focus on improving her skills as a homemaker before taking on new challenges, she wondered aloud if the school division needed a new Sex Education consultant. I made a face and said, "That's not even something to joke about."

"Who's joking?" she replied, hurrying off to look up the superintendent's phone number.

She's not half as funny as she thinks she is.

• • • • •

This evening after dinner, Jerry showed up at my front door with a very joyful look on his face. Apparently, Janine's auntie volunteers as a part-time kitchen woman at the Mission and she told him all about her young niece's generous classmate who was planning to donate $15 of his own money as well as all the money he'd collected masquerading as a squeegee kid. Jerry clasped his hands together and said, "I just knew she was talking about you! You must have been so distracted by your fungal infection last Saturday morning that you forgot to give it to me." When I tried to tell Jerry that he had it all wrong, he said that Mrs. Schultz's beautiful niece would be very disappointed to hear that. He smiled sympathetically and asked, "Is she as popular as Mrs. Schultz says she is?" I snarled that she was, and stomped up to my room to fetch the money. On my way down, I decided to hold back a little something for myself, but Jerry took one look at the pile of coins and bills in his hand and said, "That's strange! Mrs. Schultz said that you'd earned $12.45 as a squeegee kid and I only see $7.20 here," so I had no choice but to fork it all over.

Now I'm broke — again! And it's all Jerry's fault — again!

This guy is really getting on my nerves.

• • • • •

Missy Shoemaker constructed a working model of the solar system as her final project in the "Our Solar System" science unit. I was not at all impressed, because there was a sign on the bottom of her contraption that said, "NOT TO SCALE." I pointed it out to several of the lads who were hanging around the lockers and we all had a good laugh, because what good is a model if the scale is all wrong?

"Who's the bonehead now?" I asked Missy, and she said that I was, because if the model had been made to scale, Mercury would have had to be the size of a pea and Jupiter would have had to be the size of a football field. The fellows and I had a good laugh over that, too, because everyone knows that Jupiter is much larger than a football field.

Missy folded her arms and waited for us to stop acting like morons. It took quite a while, but at last she was able to hold my attention for long enough to ask me the topic of my final project. When I wouldn't tell her, she said, "It probably has something to do with jock itch." She said she knew that I was the one who wrote the question about jock itch because she recognized the curlicues in the handwriting. Everyone in the hallway had a good laugh at my expense, and when the laughter subsided, Missy asked, "How long have you had pubic lice?" This got everyone going again, especially Lyle Filbender, who began aggressively scratching his groin, pretending to be me with pubic lice. I wasn't exactly sure what pubic lice were, but instead of revealing my ignorance to a man-eater like Missy Shoemaker, I called her an insufferable cow. She called me a pubic lice, said, "I'm telling" and marched away.

Later, I was called to Miss Thorvaldson's desk for

calling Missy Shoemaker a cow. To my surprise, I was given the opportunity to explain my actions. I told Miss Thorvaldson that Missy Shoemaker had called me a pubic lice and pointed out that this was a much worse name than cow, because as far as I could tell it implied that I was a small, disgusting venereal disease insect, while a cow was at least a vertebrate. To my further surprise, Miss Thorvaldson agreed that calling me a pubic lice was inappropriate (I felt highly thankful that she didn't consider me a small, disgusting venereal disease insect, since this is usually how she treats me), but she said that she didn't consider it appropriate to call a person a cow, either. Calling Missy Shoemaker up to the front, she made us apologize and shake hands to show that there were no hard feelings. I did this, even though I still had plenty of hard feelings, because pretending that you get along with people you despise is the mature thing to do. On the way back to our desks, however, I whispered to Missy, "You shake hands like a construction worker," and she retorted, "You shake hands like a fairy princess." So you see that the facade of camaraderie was quickly shattered. World peace often faces similar problems, I understand.

I can't wait until I get an A+ on my final project — "Planet Earth: My World, My Rules" — and Missy Shoemaker is left eating my dust. Winning intellectual battles is the civilized way to crush your enemies.

•••••

All this talk about jock itch, pubic lice and scratching has obviously sunk into my subconscious, because I've been plagued by an unbearably itchy groin these past few days. Perhaps I should think about changing into

 Tape #2

a fresh pair of underwear at some point. Then again, I wouldn't want my mother to think that I've taken her intrusive little speech on pubic hygiene to heart.

Sometimes there are no easy answers.

•••••

I got an F on my solar system project. Miss Thorvaldson said that "Planet Earth: My World, My Rules" was nothing more than a rambling piece of fantasy. I was deeply offended by the accuracy of her analysis, and blamed my parents for burdening me with so many extracurricular obligations. I explained that between volunteering at the Mission and doing my paper route, I barely had time to watch my television programs. I shook my head in exasperation and said, "Where in heaven's name am I supposed to find time for schoolwork?" Miss Thorvaldson fluffed the wisps of her tinted pixie cut and rasped, "I'm sure I don't know, but you're going to have to find time or fail Science." Since I don't see science playing a major role in my life, I immediately agreed to accept a failing grade.

"That is not an option," she snapped. I tried to point out that she'd presented it as one, but she gritted her teeth really hard and sent me to my desk.

For a teacher, she sure doesn't have much patience.

•••••

Apparently Miss Thorvaldson called my parents to let them know about my dismal mark, because today when I got home from school, I was greeted at the door by my mother, who said that she'd been shocked to learn the bad news, particularly after all those hours I'd spent studying in my room. I said, "I know!" and suggested that we look into getting a high school cheerleader to tutor me. My mother said, "Perhaps." Then she whipped out my *Playboy* magazine and cried, "THEN AGAIN, PERHAPS YOU SHOULD STOP READING PORNOGRAPHY WHEN YOU'RE SUPPOSED TO BE STUDYING!"

A million thoughts went through my mind at once, but then I noticed Electra Donovan giving me a come-hither look from the front cover, so I just sighed and gazed back at her. I don't know how long I would have stared if my mother hadn't rolled up the magazine and thwacked me on the head with it. I told her, "Quit that!" and also, "Why were you going through my stuff, anyway?" but she just thwacked me again and told me that I was to stay in my room until supper.

Later, I snuck out to look for my *Playboy* magazine, but all I could find was my father lounging in the den reading the *Encyclopedia Britannica*. He was so enthralled that he didn't even notice me standing there until I pointed out that he was holding the book upside down.

Imagine being able to read a big book like that upside down! My father is a real scholar.

●●●●●

Daryl Flick was very upset to learn that his *Playboy* magazine got confiscated and declared me cut off until further notice. I shouted, "No, Daryl, no!" and promised I'd do anything to win back the privilege of free porn.

"Anything?" he asked.

I nodded fervently and said, "Yes, anything!"

He's going to think about this and get back to me. I am keeping my fingers crossed!

•••••

Tonight I called up Mr. Fitzgerald, my personal over-lord at the *Winnipeg Daily News*, to inform him that in exactly two weeks, he will no longer have access to my services.

"I am failing several subjects at school," I explained. "And although I feel this is primarily a result of being unfairly evaluated by a teacher who has it in for me for no good reason, my mother seems to think it's because I need to study more, so I'm not going to have time for your crummy paper route anymore."

The minute the words were out of my mouth, I realized how harsh they sounded, so I added, "Don't take it personally," and kindly explained to Mr. Fitzgerald that although a career in the newspaper delivery business was nothing to be ashamed of for a person like him, I, myself, found it neither rewarding nor challenging. He didn't seem very soothed by my words, however, and he didn't sound sad that I was leaving, either. In fact, he sounded downright nasty about the whole thing, and even laughed in my ear when I asked if there would be a going-away party for me. I guess that means there probably won't be one.

No big surprise there. Mr. Fitzgerald never tried very hard to make me feel welcome in the first place.

•••••

This afternoon, John Michael and I went over to Daryl Flick's house because we wanted to hang out without any mothers breathing down our necks and Daryl's mother is almost never home. I said, "You have no idea how lucky you are," but suggested that he get his mother to go shopping a little more often because there was nothing in the cupboard but a can of artichoke hearts. "How does she expect you to entertain without Ding Dongs?" I asked. In response, he threw me onto the filthy carpet and bounced up and down on my chest until I apologized.

Afterward, he said he'd thought of a way for me to get my porn privileges back. Apparently he's had it with Marv chasing him off the boulevard when he's trying to hang out with the squeegee kids. He wants to pull a prank that will make Marv look like an idiot in front of his paying customers and he wants me to help him do it. As Marv's future fellow business owner, I was reluctant at first, but then Daryl showed me a copy of *Voluptuous Vixens* and said, "Are you sure about that?" I had to hang my head and admit, "I'm not so sure about that at all."

I am a slave to my addiction.

●●●●●

I finished the last day of my paper route! No more early mornings, no more Mr. Miller and his impossible expectations. As a special treat to myself, I even wrote "UP YOURS" on the top corner of Mr. Miller's paper, though I didn't sign my name. Only a fool would be that obvious.

Best of all, however, is the fact that when Mr. Fitzgerald called to remind me to turn in my bag, he said that if I ever needed a reference, I should give him a call. His exact words were, "Kid, I want to make sure your next employer knows all about you." I was terribly flattered but said that while I appreciated his generous offer, I probably wouldn't bother following up on it. "A reference

from a person in charge of paper carriers doesn't carry much weight in the real world, you know."

Still, an employment reference! Maybe I misjudged Mr. Fitzgerald, after all — and maybe, in the end, he realized that he'd misjudged me, as well. A good lesson for us both, I guess.

•••••

Our school is having an "All Nations, All Religions Holiday Performance Evening" for Christmas. Normally, junior high school students aren't required to participate in such drivel, but the drama and music departments are on the government chopping block again and our principal is hoping that an over-the-top extravaganza involving every student in the school will show what a terrible mistake it would be to cut these departments.

My class has been assigned the job of acting out the Nativity Scene. The minute I heard the news, I asked to be excused from participating on the grounds that it would be an affront to my parents, who are committed to raising me as a godless heathen. Miss Thorvaldson denied my request, saying, "You've only been assigned to the choir, anyway." I was shocked — I said that forced participation is tantamount to religious persecution!

"Don't the religious practices of godless heathens deserve the same respect as those of anyone else?" I asked. I also demanded to know why I hadn't been considered for a speaking part. Instead of answering, Miss Thorvaldson herded me back to my desk as though I were a wayward cow. It was very humiliating, especially when Missy Shoemaker mooed at me.

I wonder if my parents are going to be as shocked as I am about the whole situation. Probably. They're always harping at me about religious tolerance when I make insensitive comments concerning the crazy practices of people profiled on *National Geographic* specials. They are real fanatics that way.

● ● ● ● ●

My mother didn't exhibit the moral outrage I'd anticipated when I explained to her about Miss Thorvaldson not respecting the fact that I'm an atheist. In fact, she only stopped scrubbing the floor long enough to give me a snippy lecture about putting the top on the blender the next time I make myself a milkshake. I waited until she finished nagging, then asked if she'd heard what I said about the Christmas concert. In response, she handed me the Spic and Span. Not even a hint of moral outrage! I can't stand people who are so caught up in their own petty problems that they can't consider my feelings.

● ● ● ● ●

This morning before class started, I asked Miss Thorvaldson if she had reconsidered her position with respect to atheists and Christmas concerts, but she just told me to get out of her parking space, where I was lying in protest. I even had a sign taped to my body that said, "BAN RELIGIOUS PERSECUTORS LIKE MISS THORVALDSON." Quite a crowd had gathered to witness the spectacle and I was hoping that the beautiful Lori Anderson of CTY television might pop by to give my cause a broader viewing audience, but no such luck. Journalists! Plenty of time for tyrants on the other side of the world, no time for tyrants on the home front.

Anyway, my plan was to keep lying in Miss Thorvaldson's parking space until I'd rallied enough support from the crowd to roll her car into the ditch in

order to teach her a lesson about being intolerant toward others. However, when she slowly started driving in on top of me, I had no choice but to scurry out of the way. I was so shocked by her reckless behavior that I pounded on the hood of her car as hard I could and shouted, "You could have killed me!" She didn't seem nearly as concerned about that as she did about the fact that I may have dented the hood of her vintage Volkswagen Beetle, and though I tried to explain that I'd been at the mercy of my boiling moral outrage when I attacked her vehicle, she couldn't find it in her heart to show me even the tiniest shred of compassion.

Some people just don't understand about boiling moral outrage, I guess.

• • • • •

Today in rehearsal I told the Virgin Mary to bite me because it wasn't the Virgin Mary at all, it was Missy Shoemaker. I was feeling irritated that she got the lead role in the Christmas concert while I was relegated to the lowly choir, so as I walked by to take my place with the other heavenly host, I gave the manger a good kick, knocking the Cabbage Patch Baby Jesus right onto the floor, head first. The Virgin Mary said, "Screw you" and called me a jerk, and that's when I told her to bite me. Then I gave her doll another kick, which sent it hurtling off the edge of the stage. Unfortunately, this alerted Miss Thorvaldson to what was going on because the flying Christ child smacked her right in the back of the head. She let out a sharp bark and turned around with an evil eye, and though I tried to say that Missy had flung the doll at me and I'd simply deflected it with my foot, Miss Thorvaldson didn't believe me.

Later, when she came to retrieve me from the office, I said it was typical of her to believe the Virgin Mary instead of me. I also tried to express how disappointed I was that she hadn't made the slightest effort to understand the symbolism of my gesture, but she just snapped, "Quiet! You're giving me a headache," straightened the jacket of her power suit and lumbered off to phone my mother.

• • • • •

I asked the second Wise Man to spit on the Virgin Mary during our next rehearsal as a personal favor to me, but he refused.

And I thought we were friends.

• • • • •

This evening, right after Daryl Flick called to tell me he'd just stolen the latest *Voluptuous Vixens* from Marv's gas station convenience store, my grandmother called to needle my father about November sales at the House of Toilets. After he got off the phone and his pulse rate returned to normal, my father gave a touching speech to my mother and me about how much he appreciated our support as he struggled to make a success of the business that would one day be mine. Then he surprised me with my own BISOB jersey and a small certificate stating that I was an official member of the Junior BISOB organization.

"I was going to save these for Christmas," he said, beaming at me. "But I'm so proud to have my only son join the BISOB team that I just couldn't wait."

I now face a terrible dilemma. How am I supposed to fulfill my promise to Daryl and participate in a prank to humiliate Marv, when, as president of BISOB, Marv

just happens to be the person who signed my beautiful new certificate? On the one hand, I am eager to step into the heady world of big business, but on the other hand, I am aching to see that new *Voluptuous Vixens*.

I have no idea what I'm going to do.

• • • • •

This morning at the Mission, I told Jerry that I was facing a wrenching personal dilemma and he was very sympathetic. He told me not to worry because whatever happened, it was part of God's plan. When I reminded him that I was an atheist and that God's plan was meaningless to me, he replied, "God loves and cares for us all, even atheists. If you pray, I'm sure He will answer your prayers." I asked Jerry, if this was true, why didn't he pray to God that there would be no more poverty? He laughed and said, "Just because God answers our prayers doesn't mean He gives us the answers we're looking for."

"How convenient for Him," I said, as Jerry hurried off to help a woman and her two small children carry their trays to a table. "I'll be sure to remember that excuse the next time I fail one of Miss Thorvaldson's math tests."

• • • • •

I just promised God that if He fixes it so that I can help Daryl without affecting my status as a member of the Junior BISOB organization, I would henceforth be an active and enthusiastic participant in His Christmas concert. I also apologized for booting Baby Jesus into Miss Thorvaldson's head (though I pointed out that it had only been a Cabbage Patch doll named Clive and that the Virgin Mary had really been asking for it). Finally, I told Him that I know all about His little trick of giving people the opposite of what they ask for and said, "If that is Your plan in this case, You can just forget it. I am a straight shooter and I expect the same from the People I deal with."

I didn't get an immediate response from Him, but since I am an atheist, I'm probably at the back of the bus when it comes to getting my prayers answered. Still, I think God will think I am the kind of guy He can respect. I had a request, I made it, and I offered Him something that He values in exchange. If this works, I may start my own religion. With a direct line to God, I would get the best television ratings of all.

• • • • •

This morning at breakfast, my father took back my BISOB jersey and certificate and apologized if it seemed as though he was trying to pressure me into playing a more active role in supporting the House of Toilets. He clapped his hand on my shoulder and said, "Son, as your mother pointed out to me last night after you'd gone to bed, you'll be a man with adult responsibilities all too soon. For now, we just want you to focus on having a regular childhood and enjoying the same kinds of experiences as every other boy your age."

After I finished chewing my mouthful of Lucky Charms, I thanked him for realizing how insensitive he'd been for putting me on the spot that way. Inside, however, I was thinking that enjoying the same kinds of experiences as every other boy my age could only mean one thing: *Voluptuous Vixens!*

If this isn't a sign from God, I don't know what is.

•••••

Daryl says he's having a hard time coming up with the perfect prank to pull on Marv. I said, "Maybe it's a sign from God that He wants you to stop all this nonsense and just give me my porn." Daryl seemed to give this serious consideration, then replied, "Maybe it's a sign that He thinks you're a bonehead," and hung up.

I think it's safe to say that Daryl doesn't know the first thing about interpreting His signs.

•••••

I was so enthusiastic during Christmas concert rehearsal today that Miss Thorvaldson had to pull me aside and ask me to stop drowning out the rest of the choir.

"I'll try," I said. "But we all have our own personal styles and mine is to sing at the top of my lungs at all times."

She looked at me suspiciously, and I could tell that she thought I was being an uncooperative atheist again, so I quickly explained how God had intervened in a wrenching personal dilemma and how I was just paying him back.

"I thought you didn't believe in God," she said.

"Who am I to argue with results?" I replied.

Later, I was just barely able to ignore the Virgin Mary when she loudly pointed out that my fly was open and she could see my dirty blue gitch. All the shepherds and their flocks had a good laugh over this one, but I simply told them, "I Forgive You" and also, "Be Prepared," because these were some of Jesus' favorite mottos, and I thought God would like the touch. In response, the Virgin Mary made a demonic pig face at me by pushing her nose up and pulling the flaps of skin under her eyes down. She looked hideous, and I had many excellent insults I could have hurled at her, but I didn't say a word.

No wonder there are so many fair-weather Christians. Real religious commitment requires a major personality overhaul and is a big pain in the butt, besides.

•••••

We had the final dress rehearsal for the Christmas concert today. It went well, though I have to admit that I'm not one of the better-dressed heavenly hosts. Lately, my mother has developed this attitude problem where she feels it appropriate to foist some of her maternal chores — such as whipping up a last-minute costume — onto me. So, instead of having a crisp white cotton robe trimmed in gold tinsel like everyone else in the choir, I have my father's old bathrobe, which has yellowed with age and has a big coffee stain down the front. Truth be told, I don't look much like a heavenly host at all, unless I'm one of Jerry's ragged street people being a heavenly host after a night of hard drinking. I think this is probably why I've been switched from my place of honor directly in front of Miss Thorvaldson, to the farthest, darkest corner of the top row. I don't mind, though, because I now get to lead my row into position. I also get an excellent view of the stage, which is good, because although Miss Thorvaldson likes us to watch her at all times to make sure we get our cues right, I prefer to compromise by watching her only when I can't find something more interesting to look at.

This is why I miss the beginnings and endings of most songs, I guess, and how I learned that my voice really booms when I'm singing by myself. I'm surprised I wasn't chosen for a solo.

• • • • •

I sprained my ankle at the Christmas concert last night, but I'm pretty sure it wasn't God's way of demonstrating His irritation with me for not paying enough attention during His concert. For one thing, I don't think that a merciful God would do such a thing, and for another, flinging a person off the end of a choir bench is not a very spectacular gesture, and He has to know that spectacular gestures are a must for the TV generation.

After the concert, Miss Thorvaldson said that I wouldn't have made such a spectacle of myself if I'd been watching where I was walking instead of blowing kisses to the audience. In response, I repeated Jerry's wise words about it all being a part of God's plan. I said, "You don't think you know better than God, do you?" Then I gave her a sorrowful look as though even I — a godless heathen — couldn't believe the sacrilege.

• • • • •

Daryl's cousin, the vicious gang member, thinks we should shoot out the windows in the gas station convenience store in order to teach Marv a lesson. He told Daryl he could get us a gun, no problem.

"You're not actually thinking of doing it, are you?" I asked Daryl, flabbergasted. "Because I won't be a part of anything like that — not for you, not even for porn!" When he snickered, "What are you, chicken?" I cried, "Yes, absolutely!" and he reluctantly admitted that he was, too.

What a relief! Daryl may be a bit of a hooligan, but it's good to know he's no criminal.

• • • • •

This weekend, John Michael and I took his little sister, Lucy, to the mall to visit Santa Claus. I haven't visited Santa for years, because most shopping mall Santas I've met really sit in judgment of a person's wish list. They say things like "That's a pretty big gift for such a little boy!" and "Easy-Bake Ovens are for girls," and I just don't need that kind of pressure at this time of year.

Still, I have as much Christmas spirit as the next guy, so I agreed to help John Michael schlepp Lucy to the mall. We had to wait in line forever, of course, and Lucy was so excited she wouldn't stop fidgeting. On several occasions, I tried to tell her that society doesn't think much of women who lift their skirts over their heads in public, but she just kept calling me a poop, so I finally said, "Takes one to know one." Then I ignored her, because I was not about to sink to the level of a three year old.

At long last, the elves took Lucy up. I was just telling John Michael how glad I was that this ordeal was almost over, when the elves returned and informed us that Lucy wanted us to be in the picture with her. I said, "Not interested," and tried to return to my conversation, but Santa pulled out a megaphone and blasted us with some jolly words of encouragement. I tried to hide, but Santa called, "I SEE YOU BEHIND THAT GIANT CANDY CANE," and boomed that there was nothing to be afraid of.

"Maybe it's you who's afraid!" I shouted, shaking my fist at him, but as I saw no graceful way out, I turned to tell John Michael that we'd better get it over with, only to discover ... he was gone!

In a panic, I tried to explain that I had to go find my friend, but two elves grabbed me by the arms and dragged me up to Santa, who rang his bells in my face and wrestled me to his free knee. He held me there while he and Lucy smiled for the camera, and as soon as the flash went off, the crowd burst into a spontaneous round of applause. I was mortified, and to make matters much, much worse, as I was getting off Santa's knee, I saw Missy Shoemaker in the front row with a huge smile on her face, clapping her heart out. I gave her the finger, of course. When Santa saw this, he snatched away my free candy cane and said that little boys like me only got lumps of coal in their stockings. "You smell like beer," I replied, dragging Lucy away by one arm before Santa could accost me further.

Eventually, I found John Michael eating a taco in the food court. I gave him my best injured look so that he would realize how deeply his betrayal had wounded me, but he must not have picked up on my nonverbal signals, because he wouldn't stop laughing.

In the future, I guess I'll have to be more direct when sharing my feelings with him.

● ● ● ● ●

Missy Shoemaker told everyone in class that I had my picture taken with Santa Claus, except in her version of the story I kept calling out, "I wuv you, Santa!" and it took three elves to drag me off him. She also said she overheard me telling him that I want My Little Pony for Christmas. I vehemently denied this, assuring my classmates that I want a machine gun and some gray underwear for Christmas, because I am a guy, and also because there isn't much you can do with My Little

Pony except braid its tail.

I guess I set that record straight.

•••••

With less than a week to go before the start of vacation, I am having more trouble than usual paying attention in class, but today I managed to focus for just long enough to pick Theodore Pinker for the holiday gift exchange. Theodore is the tallest boy in our class — already over six feet — and he is very sensitive about his abnormal height. I know this because he has terrible posture on account of slouching down to try to fit in with the rest of us and also because I once referred to him as a big oaf in gym class and he hurled the dodgeball at me so hard that it knocked the wind out of me. Later, when I told him it was very unsportsman-like to aim for my diaphragm that way, he put my underwear into the ventilation duct in the ceiling and walked out of the change room. I implored the other lads to climb on each other's backs in order to retrieve my shorts, but they laughed and laughed and then left me standing there all alone, naked from the waist down. Eventually, I had no choice but to get dressed without my underwear and I ended up chafing my package on the roughly finished inner seams of my tweed pants. Believe me, it is not a feeling I will soon forget.

At any rate, I will have to give some thought to Theodore Pinker's gift — though not too much thought, because he did cause my gonads to be rubbed raw that time. You can't cause another person's gonads to be rubbed raw and expect him to feel large amounts of inspiration on your behalf.

•••••

I had my last session before the holidays with my fine-looking psychologist, Dr. Anderson. For Christmas, I bought her a mug at Gags Unlimited that says, "DOCTORS DO IT CLINICALLY," and I stuffed it with a pair of nude pantyhose and a tube of Passion Fever lipstick. Miss Thorvaldson will receive a similar mug, only hers will say, "TEACHERS DO IT WITH CLASS," and will contain a Miss Piggy holiday brooch that lights up when you press the snout. Not only is it a stunning accessory, it is one filled with meaning, because Miss Piggy is a full-figured, fashion-conscious female who doesn't take crap from anyone, and so is Miss Thorvaldson.

Anyway, Dr. Anderson seemed very surprised by my gift. I said, "Don't be silly!" and asked if she'd gotten me a little something, as well. She said she hadn't, and asked me several questions about appropriate behavior. Instead of answering, I suggested that her New Year's resolution be to come up with a different topic for our sessions. I explained that I'd learned everything I was going to learn about appropriate behavior and that this was as appropriate as it was going to get. Then I said, "Why don't you try on your nude pantyhose and Passion Fever lipstick for me?" She refused and told me our session was over.

As I was leaving, I noticed that Dr. Anderson seems to be aging rapidly. She always looks very tired after our sessions, and I think her hair is starting to go gray. She should start taking better care of herself, because once her looks go, she'll have nothing to fall back on but her personality and intelligence, and how far will that get a woman in today's world?

•••••

Janine Schultz gave me a patch of knitting for the holiday gift exchange. She said that she'd knitted it herself and that it *was* going to be a scarf but she'd run out of time. I said, "Oh," and asked what I was supposed to do with it.

"Maybe use it as a wall decoration," she suggested. "Or a potholder."

I pointed out that it had too many snarls to be a wall decoration, and that potholders were for women, but I thanked her anyway. She fairly glowed at these kind words. It is obvious that she still adores me, though this being the case, you'd think she'd have gotten me a more impressive gift.

My gift to Theodore Pinker was a LifeSavers Storybook, although I had to remove three packages of LifeSavers from it because it'd cost more than three dollars, and Miss Thorvaldson had given us a clear three-dollar limit on gifts. Theodore was very ungracious when he discovered this. He called me "cheap" and also "a weasel." When I tried to explain that I'd acted in the best interests of not inciting jealousy and mayhem among our classmates, he tore into a pack of rum 'n' butter and crushed several between his teeth in a display of primal rage, so I didn't bother adding that he'd neglected to thank me for my gift. Sometimes it's better to just walk away.

Since it was the last day of class, I gave Miss Thorvaldson her Christmas gift. Boy, was she surprised! She tried protesting that I shouldn't have, but I gave her giant shoulder a warm squeeze and said, "Pshaw! Christmas is a time for giving — even to those who have treated us shabbily in the past." She hardly knew what to say after that, except "Happy Holidays" and "Thank goodness it's early dismissal."

●●●●●

Ah, freedom! Two weeks unburdened by the demands of the public education system. I'm going to lie around the house, eat large amounts of junk food and watch as much television as humanly possible. I will be short-tempered and cranky on account of my lack of activity and excessively high blood sugar. I will needle my mother continuously about my feelings of boredom, though I will resist any attempt by her to force me outside for some fresh air. I will grow increasingly sluggish and spend large parts of my day dozing on the couch until finally, in the end, I will feel as though the holidays have once again sped by without my having accomplished anything of value whatsoever.

It may not sound glamorous, but for me, it's tradition.

●●●●●

My mother forced me to go to the Holy Light Mission this morning, my first day of holidays. I tried to remind her about our cherished tradition of me not getting any fresh air for two whole weeks, but she said, "Things change," and booted me out the door.

Naturally, I was in a foul mood when I arrived and it was not at all improved when Jerry sent me to help load hampers into the cars of the Christmas Cheer Board volunteers who were in a frenzy to see that every person in the city had a decent meal on Christmas Day. I said things like "Relax!" and "Watch the hair" and "My back is killing me," but they just kept loading me up like some kind of pack mule.

"There isn't a moment to lose if we hope to deliver

all the hampers in time!" cried a man in a Winnipeg Jets hockey jersey, heaving a twenty-pound bag of potatoes at me.

I really think I would have lost my temper if Daryl Flick hadn't shown up partway through the morning. I knew he could only be looking for me, so I snuck up behind him and shouted, "BOO!" After he finished body slamming me into a stack of hampers, I pulled him aside to complain about the Christmas Cheer do-gooders who were so bent on helping the poor that they wouldn't let me sit down for forty-five lousy minutes. He said, "What a bunch of bums." Then he advised me to be ready to pull the prank on Marv right after Christmas. When I inquired as to the nature of the prank, he told me to mind my own business, so I settled for asking if I could expect to spend time in a juvenile detention facility afterward. In response, he grabbed my hood strings and galloped me into one of the do-gooders, who told me to get back to work before she reported me to Jerry.

After I finished with the hampers, I informed everyone that there would be no more me to kick around after today because my punishment only required me to perform selfless charity work until Christmas. Jerry urged me to reconsider, pointing out that real charity begins when you give of your own free will. I laughed and rolled my eyes, then said I'd be thinking of him when I ripped open my many gifts on Christmas Day.

"What are you hoping to get?" I asked as I pulled on my jacket.

"God's love and forgiveness," he replied, turning my collar right side out for me.

God's love and forgiveness. That Jerry. What a character!

•••••

Other than the hundred dollars my grandmother sent me, I'm sad to report that this year's Christmas haul was rather dismal. Once again, people missed my hints about wanting a big-screen television for my bedroom. Instead, my parents got me a boom box, a new velour shirt and a gift certificate entitling me to a crash course in traditional Ukrainian Dance. Aunt Maud got me a book called *The Feminine You*, about how to stay in touch with my softer side during the tumultuous time of puberty, and Ruth knitted me a thick fisherman's sweater with a matching tam. I thanked Aunt Maud but told Ruth I didn't know many boys who wore tams. She pointed out that her little Sparky is a boy and looks smashing in tams.

"Sparky is a dog," I replied, but she glared at me so ferociously that I let it drop.

The saddest news is that my mother won't even let me spend my hundred dollars on whatever I want. She said it wasn't right to just fritter away that much money, so it was going into the bank unless I could think up a suitable big-ticket item to spend it on. I racked my brains for a way to make fried chicken and porn sound like big-ticket items. When I came up empty, she said, "Well, what about a chemistry set, or a pair of hockey skates?" I threw up my hands in despair.

Sometimes it's like living with a stranger.

•••••

By the way, have you noticed how calm I'm being about the Ukrainian dance lessons? I must still be in shock.

• • • • •

I tried to rationally discuss my gift certificate from hell with my parents, but they got their noses out of joint the minute I referred to it as my gift certificate from hell.

"Really, son! Have you forgotten that I was a member of the Rusalka Ukrainian Dance Ensemble for almost six years?" asked my father. "Give it a chance! Think of the moves you'll be able to show off at your next school dance."

I pictured myself twirling around the gym in red baggy pants and a sequined vest.

"I don't think so," I told him. "Can't we take it back — or rip it up? Please?"

My mother refused to do either of these things but agreed not to make me take the lessons right away. "You can cash in the certificate anytime you want," she said, leaning over to give me a hug.

"How about the first of never?" I suggested, cranking up the volume on my boom box. The music was too loud for me to hear her reply, but from the look on her face, I got the feeling it wasn't pretty.

• • • • •

This afternoon my mother made me go tobogganing with John Michael and Daryl Flick, and I'm now lying on my bed with her entire stockpile of frozen Salisbury steaks packed around my body in order to keep the swelling down. I'm certain I wouldn't be suffering so badly if only Daryl had stayed on his scrap of cardboard and left me to enjoy my giant inner tube in peace, but the minute he and John Michael saw what a terrific ride my tube was, they jumped in on top of me. I spent the entire afternoon careening down the icy slope at the bottom of the heap with my backside wedged into the hole of the tube, begging Daryl not to steer us toward the large bump at the bottom of the hill. His only response was to laugh like a maniac as we hit the bump and flew into the air, and if I didn't land on some portion of my skull, my spine absorbed the full impact of our crash landing. Afterward, the two of them scrambled back up the hill — leaving me to drag up the inner tube — and the one time I thought Daryl was returning to assist me to my feet, he just kicked snow in my face and excitedly shouted, "Hurry it up!"

I think I will lend Daryl *The Feminine You*. He really needs to get in touch with his softer side.

• • • • •

I told my parents that I'm meeting John Michael for a twilight game of street hockey this evening, but in reality I'm meeting Daryl in the empty lot beside the Mission. Yesterday after tobogganing, he finally told me his big plan for Marv. It seems that I'm supposed to go into the gas station convenience store tonight and distract Marv while Daryl props a bucket of freezing water on the ledge above the front door and then tips over the garbage pails by the gas pumps. When I see that he's done this last part, I'm supposed to say, "Oh, no, Marv! It looks like someone's been going through your garbage again!" Daryl figures that when Marv rushes outside with his baseball bat to investigate, the bucket will tip and soak him from head to toe, not only making him look ridiculous, but possibly giving him a cold, as well.

As soon as Daryl finished explaining all this, I said, "That's it? Three weeks and the best you can do is the old bucket-of-water-over-the-door trick? Could you possibly have come up with something less original?"

"Who cares about original?" he replied. "That jerk won't even let me in his store no more, and he's going to get what he's got coming to him."

I tried to suggest several refinements to the plan, but Daryl toppled me backward into my giant inner tube, pinned me beneath his scrap of cardboard and refused to let me up until I stopped talking.

At least I will get my porn privileges back for doing nothing more than playing the role of an innocent bystander. It could have been worse.

• • • • •

Can't talk except to say that the prank on Marv went horribly awry! The bucket must have tipped before Daryl could get it onto the ledge ... the water spilled and froze ... Marv ran out and slipped — once on the ice, and a second time on his own bat, which he'd dropped while clawing for a handhold in a futile effort to keep from going down the first time! Now he's been rushed to the hospital with a bloody head wound and — Oh! Got to go! Someone's coming!

• • • • •

It was just my mother with a mug of warm milk and plateful of cream puff pastries from the Blue Moon Café, which I can't even eat because I feel sick to my stomach. Oh, the irony! I haven't talked to Daryl yet, and I'm afraid to call him because my mother keeps barging in on me every two seconds to make sure I'm not going into shock from the trauma of having to call the ambulance for Marv and give a statement to the police.

I can't believe this is happening to me.

• • • • •

It's three in the morning. I just got off the phone with Daryl. He answered on the first ring — he couldn't sleep, either, I guess. It sounded like he'd been crying, but when I tried to ask if he had, he swore at me and blew his nose, so instead I asked what happened to the plan. He explained that his hands had been so cold that he'd fumbled the bucket before he could get it into position and that he hadn't been able to warn me because Marv had said he'd call the cops if Daryl ever set foot in his store again.

"I didn't mean for him to get hurt, you know," he said. "I just wanted to teach him a lesson."

"I know," I replied.

We sat there feeling guilty together until Daryl finally spoke again, this time in a voice so low that I could barely hear him.

"I guess there's no point in us both getting caught," he whispered. "So I've been thinking: since you didn't really do nothing they can get you for, you should probably just save yourself."

Well, it goes without saying that saving myself had been at the forefront of my thoughts since that first wretched moment Marv hit the ice slick, but when Daryl suggested it, he sounded so dejected that I had a sudden, inexplicable change of heart. I said, "What are you talking about?" and pledged, there and then, to stand by him — my friend! — come what may.

"Don't be a moron," he replied, but he said it with that old, familiar Daryl spirit, and I knew he was relieved not to have to face this thing alone.

Before we hung up, I promised to keep my ear to the

ground and do everything I could to throw the coppers off our scent. I also suggested that we pray to our respective deities that Marv survive the night. Daryl agreed.

I can't believe I'm sticking by him instead of saving myself, particularly since I can legitimately claim to have been a mostly innocent bystander.

Perhaps I hit my head, too, and just don't remember doing it.

• • • • •

Hallelujah! Marv is going to be just fine except for the eight pins he needs to repair the ankle he shattered when he tripped over his bat. Felix from the pawnshop called this morning to let us know that Marv was heading into surgery. Apparently, the frightening gash I'd seen on his head had only been superficial, and while he did briefly lose consciousness at the scene, by the time the ambulance arrived at the hospital, he was in fine fettle, barking at the attendants to turn the bus around so he could go back and chase down the bum who did this to him.

As soon as my father got off the phone with Felix, I slipped up to my room and contacted God. I thanked Him profusely for answering my prayer and promised that, in the future, I would refrain from praying for things like pornography and stick to matters of life and death so as not to clog the pipeline.

I hope He appreciates the sacrifice.

• • • • •

I secretly called Daryl to tell him the good news about Marv. He had some good news for me, as well — he secretly talked to John Michael, and he's agreed to swear that both Daryl and I were playing street hockey with him between the hours of seven and nine.

Secrets and alibis — two very good reasons to have very good friends.

•••••

Mr. Filbender dropped by this evening after dinner to let us know that Marv's surgery went well, and to inform my father that Marv is convinced he was ambushed by one of Jerry's street people. It seems that about twenty minutes before Daryl and I arrived at the gas station on that fateful evening, a street person tried to use the bathroom there. When Marv told him to come back after he'd taken a shower and gotten a job, this person pitched a small fit before storming off. Marv said the fact that the ice slick was made of urine, combined with the fact that he'd seen someone lurking and laughing near the overturned garbage pails by the gas pumps, convinced him that it was the work of that smelly bum.

Thinking I must have heard wrong, I asked, "What do you mean the ice slick was made of urine?"

Mr. Filbender explained that the police had tested it and what's more, they'd managed to collect a sample containing some sloughed epithelial cells, which means that if they ever catch the perpetrator, they'll be able to make a DNA match and convict him.

"Fantastic!" I cried, inwardly cursing myself for agreeing to stand by my good-for-nothing friend.

My father frowned and said, "But I still don't understand how Marv can be sure it was the guy from earlier."

"He saw someone lurking and *laughing*," repeated Mr. Filbender. "Who else could it have been? I tell you, those people have been nothing but a problem from the moment that soup kitchen opened, and this time they've gone too far."

Before he left, Mr. Filbender handed my father an envelope containing the confidential first draft of a pending BISOB resolution. Then he praised me for sticking by Marv after that lowlife caused him injury and suggested that I consider joining the Junior BISOB organization.

"My son, Lyle, has just been elected president," he said. "I'm sure he could find a position suitable for someone like you."

Oh, I'll just bet he could.

• • • • •

I saw Daryl for the first time since the Night of Marv and the first thing I did was berate him for putting urine in the pail when the plan had clearly called for water.

"What were you thinking?" I asked. He replied that he'd been thinking it would be extra funny to see Marv soaked with piss. "It was funny just seeing him *slip* on piss," he said, chuckling, "until he saw me laughing and hurt himself trying to jump up and chase after me." I shook my head and said, "You're a real Neanderthal sometimes, you know that?" In response, he pretended to pull out his wiener and pee all over me.

I think, perhaps, that calling him a Neanderthal was an insult to Neanderthals.

• • • • •

I was in the pawnshop today trying to get Felix to take my Christmas tam. He said that although he was tempted, the bottom had recently fallen out of the orange tam market and he was going to have to take a pass.

Then he asked if I'd heard about Marv's postoperative complications. Feeling queasy, I said, "No, what's up?" He explained that Marv had acquired a nasty infection that was going to require him to extend his hospital stay by at least another two weeks.

"It hasn't done much for his temper," observed Felix, trying on my tam one last time.

No, I don't suppose it has.

•••••

My grandmother called during our end-of-holidays celebration dinner to wish us Happy New Year and to tell my father that December sales had almost met her expectations — though to be fair, she'd lowered them considerably following November's dismal performance. I said, "Way to go, Dad!" then asked my grandmother if she'd heard about Marv's accident.

"That was no accident," she declared, adding that the time was ripe to take action against "those people" for the sake of decent, hard-working folks everywhere.

After we sat back down and resumed eating, my father said, "I think everyone needs to calm down. I'm still not convinced that what happened to Marv wasn't some silly, boyish prank gone terribly wrong." This was so close to the truth that I nearly inhaled a barbecued chicken wing. After I finished choking, I said, "No one appreciates the voice of reason more than I do, Dad, but every one of your fellow BISOB members disagrees with you, and you can't afford to become a pariah in the local business community over something like this. Especially," I added, "when Grandmother is finally starting to speak of you in such glowing terms." He didn't look happy when I said this, but I guess he saw the logic in it because he finally let the subject drop.

Phew! What is it with him, fighting to keep those on the fringes of society from being falsely accused? It's almost as bad as Jerry's obsession with poverty!

• • • • •

Miss Thorvaldson got a jazzy new outfit over the holidays — a cream-colored pantsuit and blue silk blouse with a matching suede fedora. In an effort to start the new year off on the right foot, I lavished her with compliments about her ensemble. Unfortunately, she didn't seem to appreciate my kind words — not even when I said that her new outfit made her look a little like a female Lone Ranger. Instead, she ordered me to take my seat and later gave me a detention when she came back from lunch and caught me twirling my imaginary six-guns while wearing her fedora.

I guess we got off on the wrong foot, after all. Oh well, I should have expected as much. That is one woman who doesn't know how to accept a compliment.

• • • • •

Today in Family Life class, Mr. Bennet told us that this term, we are going to divide into couples and babysit an egg for a whole week in order to learn about the responsibilities of parenthood. I said I hoped this wasn't related to the exercise we did in Science where we had to package up an egg and drop it from a second story window without breaking it, because I would never do that to my own child, and plus my egg smashed to smithereens because I didn't bother to package it very well. Mr. Bennet said, "Don't worry," so then I asked if the exercise was going to include same-sex couples. When he said, "I'm not sure," I pointed out that there were probably people in this very class who were struggling with the issue of sexual orientation. I asked, "Who are we to send the message that homosexuals shouldn't be allowed to experience the miracle of life?" I think I had him there.

Later, Lyle Filbender said that only a real fruitcake would ask Mr. Bennet about same-sex couples. I told him I wasn't even a fruitcake — that I was only being realistic regarding today's definition of the family and that he was the fruitcake himself. After that, he began chasing me with a large icicle aimed directly at my heart, so I headed for the schoolyard monitor and spent the rest of the lunch hour crowding around her and mouthing to Lyle Filbender that he should bite me.

I feel sorry for whoever gets him as a partner. She and the egg will probably end up in a shelter.

• • • • •

My mother drove John Michael and me to the hospital to see Marv. He introduced me to everyone as the boy who saved him and promised me free Twinkies for life as a small token of his gratitude. I was so touched that I started to salivate.

"Marv," I said, "you are a man of unsurpassed generosity of spirit." He looked terribly pleased. Then he ordered the nurses to turn up his morphine drip and told us to leave because it was time for his sponge bath.

Free Twinkies for life! And to think that I used to believe that crime didn't pay.

• • • • •

I've been paired with Lyle Filbender for the egg exercise, and Missy Shoemaker is going to be a single mother. When I told her this should come as no surprise because she is far too brash to ever keep a man for long, she said that it was her idea to be artificially inseminated in order to avoid any unpleasant entanglements for the sake of the egg. I laughed lewdly and said, "If you're looking for a sperm donor I'd be happy to oblige," but she said she'd sooner eat dirt, so I said, "You're on your own, then!" and walked away. Missy Shoemaker can be terribly inappropriate sometimes. Imagine choosing dirt over my sperms.

Of course, Lyle Filbender is in a real state about being my partner. I told him to look on the bright side — at least I'm goodlooking! Then I said that he's really going to have to work on his temper now, since eggs are fragile and easily crushed if you smash them with your fists in a fit of rage. I also offered to lend him *The Feminine You* to help him grow into his new nurturing role, and pointed out that we're going to have to get better at conflict resolution now that we're about to become parents. He grabbed the front of his pants and grunted, "Resolve this!"

He'd better clean up his act. I don't want him behaving that way in front of my egg.

●●●●●

Our egg exercise starts on Friday, and already Lyle Filbender and I are embroiled in a bitter custody battle because neither of us wants the egg over the weekend. Mr. Bennet asked, "How do you think the egg feels about this rejection by its parents?" I said I didn't see why the egg's feelings should come before mine, and that mine were that I didn't want to be stuck with it over the weekend. When Lyle Filbender said, "I agree!" I told him how pleased I was to see him making an effort in this relationship for a change. In response, he gave me a vicious pinch and asked Mr. Bennet to be reassigned to another relationship, preferably of the heterosexual variety. I felt huffy about this, and complained, "My self-esteem is going to take a real beating if my partner keeps treating me this way, you know." I also pointed out that this was no kind of environment for an egg to grow up in, but Mr. Bennet just said, "Work it out!" and "I hope you're learning something."

In the end, I got stuck with the egg for the weekend because Lyle said he'd pound my head against a wall if I didn't take it. Already I feel resentful toward the egg.

●●●●●

Mr. Bennet handed out our eggs today. I've named mine Henry, although Lyle Filbender insists he will call him Butch. I told him this was going to be very confusing for Henry, but he replied that Butch was much smarter than I gave him credit for.

"I know exactly how smart Henry is," I said. "My boy is a genius! And I'm going to spend all weekend telling him what a cretin his other father is." Then I left the classroom without allowing Lyle Filbender to say his good-byes.

In retrospect, I probably shouldn't have used Henry as an emotional pawn that way, but Lyle Filbender really bugs me sometimes, and it was the best way I could think of to lash out at him.

●●●●●

I introduced Henry to my parents this evening, but his debut was overshadowed by the news that the latest BISOB resolution has been approved with flying colors. When I asked, "What resolution is that?" my father explained that it's a resolution to spare no effort in shutting down the Holy Light Mission.

"You mean Jerry's Mission?" I asked. "The one that feeds all those hungry people?" My father nodded uncomfortably. In an enthusiastic voice, Henry's Grandpa Filbender — who'd dropped by with the big news — added, "It was unanimous, except for one vote against! With that kind of support, I'm sure we can make this thing happen!"

Later, I privately confessed to Henry about the part I'd played in Marv's accident. He didn't say anything, but I knew what he was thinking.

"You think our little prank had something to do with this resolution, don't you?" I whispered. "You think it's my fault that Jerry's Mission is going to be shut down, don't you?"

When Henry remained silent, I said, "Stop looking at me that way." Then I ignored him for the rest of the evening.

Children can be so judgmental sometimes.

● ● ● ● ●

I saw Jerry on my way home from school today. He was arguing with some men outside the Mission — pleading with them, really. When I asked if their argument had something to do with the new BISOB resolution, they all turned and stared. Jerry asked, "What new BISOB resolution?" It was a very awkward moment for me, but I blurted, "Never mind!" and ran away, so I don't think they noticed.

Just before I was out of earshot, I heard Jerry resume pleading with the men to find shelter for the evening, because the temperature was going down to forty below.

This BISOB resolution is going to kill him.

•••••

I got kicked out of the movie theater this afternoon because of Henry, and as a punishment, I'm storing him in my gym shoe for several hours. The whole experience has really turned me off children, and eggs. If only my parents had agreed to give up their symphony tickets in order to stay home and babysit Henry! As a result of their selfishness, I had to drag him to the movie theater, where he evidently created an unseemly bulge in my coat pocket, because I was pulled aside and frisked by the ticket taker who told me, "No outside food allowed." I tried to explain that it wasn't food, it was my precious son, Henry, but there was obviously no reasoning with the guy. Just as I was walking over to chuck Henry in the garbage can, Miss Thorvaldson appeared out of nowhere and asked, "Where are you going with that egg?"

What could I do? I gave Henry a little kiss to show my deep affection for him, then turned and walked out of the theater.

•••••

I'm sad to report that when we dropped by his house today, Uncle Daryl refused to play peekaboo with Henry, and even swore when Henry tried to play tickle with him. I was filled with parental indignation, but Daryl interrupted my fiery speech about how rejection can crush a child's spirit by asking me if I wanted to go pick out the girlie magazines I'd earned by my participation in the Night of Marv.

"You bet I do!" I cried, chucking Henry onto a nearby pile of dirty laundry.

Hours later, my knapsack full of porn, I was halfway out the door when Daryl said, "What about Henry?"

"Who?" I asked.

He handed me my son.

No parent is perfect, I guess.

•••••

I had to get a new Henry from the refrigerator because my father made the original Henry into an omelet. I'd put him in with the other eggs because I'd heard it was important for adopted children from another culture to learn about their own People, and also because I was sick of him hanging around me every minute. Regardless, you can imagine my shock when I walked into the kitchen to find Henry's lifeless shell sitting on the counter next to the cheddar cheese and green onions. My father was mortified — he said that when he saw Henry sitting in the egg carton, he just assumed that my project was over. He apologized over and over again, but I said, "It's a little late for sorry, isn't it?" and asked him to please scrape the leftover Henry into the garbage when he was done.

•••••

This afternoon I handed a new Henry over to Lyle Filbender. Missy Shoemaker spied the exchange and asked, "Didn't your egg used to have blue eyes?" I told her that Henry's eyes had always been orange and suggested that she mind her own business.

"No problem," she replied. "Being the single mother of triplets doesn't leave a lot of time to waste on riffraff like you, anyway."

Triplets? I can't stand Missy Shoemaker. She is such an overachiever.

•••••

My grandmother called to ask if I was as relieved as she was about the latest BISOB resolution. When I said, "I guess," she reminded me that it was my responsibility as a future business owner to do everything I could to ensure a healthy local business climate.

"You can't be heir to the House of Toilets fortune if there is no House of Toilets, can you?" she asked. Cramming a handful of Doritos into my mouth, I mumbled that I hadn't thought of it that way.

"Well, you'd better start thinking about it that way because that's the way it is," she said sharply. "Make no mistake, child — the world is made up of those who have and those who have not, and if a body doesn't fight tooth and nail his whole life to keep what's his, it'll be gone before he can say jackrabbit." When I told her that it sounded like an awful lot of work and that I'd rather just watch TV, she didn't guffaw the way she usually does when I'm being a wiseacre. Instead, she cleared her throat and said, "When I was your age, my own mother had been dead and buried a year and I'd already learned how to divide six potatoes among eight hungry mouths. You just think about that when the time comes that you're called to action." Biting into another chip, I solemnly promised that I would, and hung up.

•••••

I've been walking the long way home these days in order to avoid bumping into Jerry. I just know that when he finds out what BISOB has planned, he's going to tell me his own sad story and say I should side with him.

Why won't everyone leave me alone? I'm anxious enough worrying about how my estranged partner is treating my only son — I don't need the added stress of being dragged into the middle of a fight that is sure to tear the community apart. Although I stand poised on the brink of manhood, technically I'm still only thirteen. The fate of the Holy Light Mission has nothing to do with me.

●●●●●

Henry came to school with an eye patch today. I was so upset that I shrieked as loud as I could, and Miss Thorvaldson made me put my head down on my desk for ten minutes. Afterward, at lunch hour, Lyle Filbender said, "Butch told me those long orange eyelashes made him feel like puking," and that our son had asked if something couldn't be done to give him a more masculine look. When I wailed, "But an eye patch!" and shook my head in despair, Lyle just said, "You don't get him until Thursday. I can do what I want with him 'til then."

I'm certain Lyle's turning Henry into a thug just to get back at me. There's no telling where this ugliness will end.

●●●●●

Henry was mortally wounded at Lyle Filbender's hockey practice last night, and at this moment he is lying in my locker wrapped in several rolls of scotch tape, leaking his innards all over my math textbook. I was grief stricken at first, but then Lyle and I discussed our options and decided that the best thing to do would be to get another new Henry, so I'm going to dispose of the leaking Henry on the way home from school and fix us up with a fresh one tonight. I even said, "I'm willing to keep the eye patch, Lyle, if you'll allow me to give the new Henry a bow tie." He wasn't too pleased, but he agreed.

It's amazing how a sick child can bring two people together. I feel close to Lyle Filbender in a way I never thought possible.

• • • • •

Apparently, Jerry has finally learned that his soup kitchen is under attack, because Janine Schultz's auntie — the one who occasionally volunteers as a kitchen woman — came to the door this evening to ask my parents to sign a petition in support of the Mission. My father apologetically explained that as a local business-man, he couldn't afford to have his name on a document like that, but offered to anonymously donate twenty dollars.

"At a time like this, your voice is more important than your money," declared Janine's auntie. "But," she added, plucking the bill from his fingers, "we'll certainly take your money."

As she was leaving, she turned to me and said, "By the way, Jerry has been wondering when you're going to come by and pledge your support. He says that with all the firsthand experience you've had helping to feed the poor, he just knows you'll want to do the right thing." I made a noncommittal grunt and slunk off to watch TV.

Maybe if I lie low for long enough, everyone will just forget about me.

• • • • •

This morning when I showed up at school, I saw Janine Schultz huddled up next to Theodore Pinker, who was using his freakishly tall frame to block the howling north wind that threatened to freeze the ears off every bonehead in the schoolyard who'd refused to wear a toque to school, which was practically all of us. She took no notice of me at all when I sauntered past, so I retraced my steps and tried again, this time holding up Henry and asking after her own little girl, Gwendolyn Rose.

"Our daughter's fine, thanks," said Theodore, putting his arm around Janine's shoulder and baring his teeth at me. Janine said nothing. I spent the last few moments before the bell rang crouched in the shelter of the school's south wall feeling strangely unsettled, but taking comfort in Henry's quiet presence.

I wonder if Janine's auntie said something about me giving Jerry the brush-off.

• • • • •

I had a session with my fine-looking psychologist, Dr. Anderson. I told her all about my devotion to Henry and asked if she had any children. When she said, "None of your business," I told her not to worry if she was infertile, because parenthood really wasn't all it was cracked up to be — although I admitted that it was easy for me to say, because I had Henry. In my most compassionate voice, I added, "Perhaps if you work hard at redirecting your maternal energies, your barren womb won't haunt you so much." She gave me a foul look and asked if I ever gave thought to the consequences of my statements before opening my mouth. Miffed, I muttered, "Nagging me is not what I meant by redirecting

your maternal energies." She ended our session early, which was all right with me. She is still fine-looking, but I'm finding her very critical these days. Perhaps our relationship is getting stale; perhaps I need a new psychologist.

Then again, perhaps she just needs to work a little harder at keeping my affections. Perhaps I will suggest this to her at my next session.

• • • • •

We handed in our eggs today because the assignment was over. Mr. Bennet asked how we'd enjoyed parenting, and like the old married couple we are, Lyle Filbender and I chorused, "It sucked!" The whole class laughed. Mr. Bennet smiled and said that parenthood can actually be a wonderful experience if you have the emotional maturity to deal with it. I shouted, "That'll be the day!" and turned to give Lyle a high five, but he didn't high five me back. I was hurt, because I thought we'd grown much closer on account of the leaking-Henry incident, so I leaned over to whisper that he really knew how to sap the joy out of a person and he burped in my face.

The class went on to discuss how fragile and precious children are, and Mr. Bennet asked if we thought that an egg was a good surrogate child. I said, "Not really," and pointed out that eggs weren't very precious at all, since you can buy twelve of them for just a few dollars. "I don't think you need to confuse matters by intro-ducing the whole issue of surrogates, either," I added. Mr. Bennet thanked me for my input, but said that his main point had been how fragile and vulnerable both eggs and children are.

"Without proper care and handling, both eggs and children can be damaged beyond repair," he said. Then he asked if any of us had damaged our eggs during the weeklong exercise. There were a lot of guilty faces, if you ask me, but only Missy Shoemaker confessed to cracking one of the triplets when its tiny, homemade flannel blanket came untucked and it rolled against the side of the Popsicle stick bassinet while she was rocking it to sleep on Tuesday night. She even admitted that it was her fault for forgetting to double-check that the blanket was securely tucked. I shouted, "Tell it to the judge!" and told Mr. Bennet that I hoped Missy Shoemaker would be reported to the authorities, and also fail the assignment.

I didn't bother to mention the several replacement Henrys, because I didn't want to distract people from the horror of Missy Shoemaker's negligence, and also because I didn't know if people would understand my motivations. It's not that I didn't like the first two Henrys, it's just that they got broken, and one of them got eaten, and I didn't want to hand Mr. Bennet back a bagful of damaged goods. Anyway, just look what people are saying about Missy Shoemaker — and her egg only got slightly fractured. Mine got completely destroyed. Twice! Imagine what they would be saying about me.

•••••

Marv was finally released from the hospital, so John Michael and I stopped in at the gas station convenience store on the way home from school today to welcome him home and hit him up for a couple of free Twinkies. While we were there, he excitedly showed us the petition he'd drawn up in support of shutting down the Mission. Nudging a pen and another package of Twinkies across the counter at me, he said, "Would you like to be the first to sign it?" I didn't really want to be the first to sign it, but decided it would feel awkward to refuse while I was gorging myself on free sponge cakes. So, licking off my fingers, I picked up the pen and quickly scrawled my signature. "Do you want to sign?" I asked John Michael, passing him the pen. He shook his head and passed the pen to Marv. I don't think Marv was too happy about that, because he narrowed his eyes at John Michael before picking up his crutches and hobbling down the counter to help a paying customer.

Later, when I asked John Michael why he'd embarrassed me in front of my Twinkie benefactor like that, he said, "Because I didn't want to sign it."

He makes it sound so simple.

$$\bullet \bullet \bullet \bullet \bullet$$

Lyle Filbender and I got an Unsatisfactory mark on our egg assignment. Mr. Bennet said the mark was a reflection of the fact that we'd lied to him about not damaging our egg. He said, "I want to send a strong message that if you're having problems coping with your child, the answer is not to hide it, but to get help." I told him I had no idea what he was talking about and said that I was a perfectly well-adjusted young parent. In response, he pointed out that the Henry we handed in was hard-boiled and the original Henry was raw, so I flew into a terrible rage and cursed the day that Henry was born. Mr. Bennet said, "This is what I'm talking about," and added that he hoped I'd be paying close attention to the lessons on birth control. I just rolled my eyes at him. He should know by now that I never pay close attention to anything.

After class, Lyle Filbender gave me a smack in the head for causing us to get an Unsatisfactory mark. I said I would have been better able to cope if he'd been a more supportive partner, but he just kicked my Adidas bag down the hall and stomped off.

I can't *tell* you how glad I am to be out of that relationship!

I knew that breast pump was
going to be trouble the minute
I applied it to my neck.
If you ask me, those things
should have a warning label.

J erry accosted me at the Blue Moon Café this afternoon, demanding to know if it was really my signature he'd seen on Marv's petition.

"What petition?" I asked innocently, not meeting his eyes.

"You know very well what petition," he replied.

I waited for him to say something more, so that I could lash out at him for trying to make me feel guilty, but he just turned on one heel and left the café without another word.

•••••

My mother got a part-time job as a lactation consultant! The day she drove John Michael and me to the hospital to visit Marv, she dropped by the human resources office to introduce herself, and the manager was so impressed by her pizzazz that he found her a job running community-based breast-feeding clinics. When she told us the good news, she said she was really looking forward to having a positive impact with a population that needs her.

"Congratulations," I replied. "But who could need you more than your family? Hot meals don't grow on trees, you know." She shrugged and said it was high time I learned my way around the kitchen, anyway.

Learned my way around the kitchen? I hope she's not suggesting what I think she's suggesting. My mother is a woman, and a mother. She derives deep, personal satisfaction from feeding and cleaning up after me. I, on the other hand, find those sorts of activities a drag. I hope she appreciates this difference in our perspectives.

•••••

Janine Schultz brought Jerry's petition to school today. She was wearing bubblegum Lipsmackers lip gloss and a button that said, "Save Our Soup Kitchen."

"Jerry said you forgot to pick yours up," she said, holding a second button out to me.

Miffed by Jerry's impertinence, I was about to ask if I looked like a walking billboard, when I suddenly remembered the way Janine had fawned over Theodore Pinker last week in the schoolyard. Hoping that Theodore was watching the mother of his child put the moves on me, I smiled warmly and said, "Why, thank you, Janine!" She smiled back as I scooped up the button and then laughed out loud when I accidentally stabbed myself in the chest while trying to pin it on. Before I could berate her for her insensitivity, however, she took the button from my hand and murmured, "Here, let me." I froze as she leaned forward, smelling of bubblegum and baby shampoo, and carefully pinned "Save Our Soup Kitchen" to the front of my shirt.

"And would you like to be the first to sign my petition?" she asked prettily, handing me a pen. My mouth hanging open, I nodded once and somehow managed to scribble my name at the top of the page.

Later, in the lunchroom, I overheard Theodore Pinker offer to wear one of Janine's buttons, too. When she said, "Sorry, Theo. I only had one extra," I permitted myself a small smile, which lingered on my lips until Theodore walked over and spat on my french fries.

All I have to say is that it's a lucky thing I eat my fries with lots of cheap ketchup. The tangy aftertaste completely covered up the taste of Theodore's spit.

●●●●●

Although I initially felt pleased at having one-upped Theodore Pinker, upon thinking it over, I've decided that I feel manipulated by Janine — and by Jerry. I can't believe they got me to sign that petition by using Janine's feminine wiles to momentarily blind me to my own indifference. It was a cheap shot.

●●●●●

I dragged John Michael over to the Mission after school to give me moral support while I chastised Jerry for siccing Janine on me that way.

"I think it was highly inappropriate for you to use my weakness for female flesh against me," I declared, as Jerry danced around, praising God for helping me to see the light.

He immediately stopped dancing and apologized for asking Mrs. Schultz to pass on my button.

"I'd *never* have done it if I'd known you found her so attractive," he exclaimed. "But she's four times your age! And completely gray! How could I have known?" When I rolled my eyes and told him that I was referring to Janine, he laughed and said Mrs. Schultz had mentioned that she might get her niece involved. "And I guess she did!" he cried, rattling his petition in my face. "Now, when can you come by and help put up signs? I hear the other side's going to try to rally the community into pressuring the city council to pull our municipal funding, and we need to fight fire with fire!" I hemmed and hawed and finally told him I'd have to check my schedule.

As we were leaving, John Michael — who'd stood by my side in dutiful silence the whole time — suddenly piped up and offered to help any way he could. Jerry

was touched, but I was annoyed, because John Michael's caring attitude made me look like an unsympathetic boor, when really I was just an uninterested one.

"What'd you do that for?" I complained after we'd said good-bye to Jerry and stepped out into the cold.

"Because I wanted to," he replied, pulling his hat down over his ears. I waited for him to offer some further explanation, but he just turned and headed for home.

John Michael has got a lot to learn about giving moral support.

• • • • •

Lyle Filbender brought the other petition to school — the one I'd signed for Marv. He waited until Miss Thorvaldson was unexpectedly called to the office after morning announcements to confront me with it.

"Isn't this your signature?" he asked. With a nervous smile at Janine, I pretended to examine it carefully before declaring it a clever forgery. "I'm sure it's your signature," he insisted loudly, winking at Theodore Pinker. "I can tell by the curlicues."

When she heard this, Janine frowned, got to her feet and edged forward for a closer look. "Let me see that again," I said, grabbing for the petition. With a wolfish grin, Lyle handed it over.

Five seconds later, it was fluttering down around his head in shreds.

By the time Miss Thorvaldson returned, Lyle was chasing me around the room at high speed, bellowing and kicking over chairs as he went. Missy Shoemaker — who'd been left in charge during Miss Thorvaldson's absence — was blowing her athletic whistle full blast in an attempt to restore order, and the rest of the class was screaming like a pack of frenzied Romans hoping to see a poor Christian (me) get devoured by a lion (Lyle). It took Miss Thorvaldson quite a while to get us all calmed down again, and even though I shared with her my excellent metaphor about me being a persecuted Christian and suggested that I'd suffered enough for one day, she persecuted me some more by giving me a detention.

Hail, Caesar.

•••••

Lyle Filbender and his gang of Junior BISOB thugs ambushed John Michael and me on our way home from school. They hid behind the rusty oil drum in the empty lot beside the Mission and when we walked by, pelted us with icy snowballs! John Michael instinctively dove for the cover of the nearest wall, but I was so shocked by the onslaught that I just stood staring like a deer caught in the headlights, which is probably why I took a direct hit to the face. The sight of my bleeding nose scattered our attackers and rendered me so hysterical that John Michael had to run and fetch Jerry. After dragging me inside, propping me up in a chair and stuffing some twisted paper towel into each nostril, Jerry called my mother, who rushed to pick me up but refused to carry me out to the car.

I'm now sitting under a warm comforter on the couch in the TV room, with a small bag of frozen peas for my injured nose and a large bag of ketchup chips for my injured emotions, listening to my parents argue over the best way to deal with Lyle Filbender's vicious attack.

I guess every cloud really does have a silver lining.

•••••

No word on Lyle Filbender's comeuppance yet, but Daryl stopped by to see how I was doing and my mother invited him to stay for dinner. He ate three helpings of her meatloaf even though I whispered that I was pretty sure she'd added sawdust, and he said he thought my swollen nose made me look tough.

"I am tough," I replied, launching into a long, complicated story about how I'd personally pulverized one attacker after another. I'd just finished describing the hairy, hulking colossus of a man who'd tried to run me down with a Harley-Davidson motorcycle, when Daryl swallowed a spoonful of canned peas and said, "John Michael told me you got hit in the face by a snowball because you forgot to duck."

"There are two sides to every story," I said wisely. Daryl shrugged and reached for another bun, but it was obvious that my comment left him wondering which version of events to believe.

•••••

Aunt Maud and Ruth found out about my bloody nose. Aunt Maud examined me carefully and suggested that I duck next time. Ruth — who'd somehow caught wind of the fact that I'd signed Jerry's petition and leaped to the conclusion that I'd been attacked for taking a stand on the issue of the soup kitchen closure — gave me a big hug and congratulated me on getting maimed for a good cause. I retorted that no cause was worth marring my chiseled good looks and that I'd have done or said just about anything to avoid disfigurement.

"And what's going to happen to the animal who did this to you?" she asked, ignoring me completely. I said I hoped to see him charged with attempted murder, particularly since this wasn't the first time he'd tried to kill me.

"You all remember the Mr. Miller fiasco, don't you?" I asked gravely. My mother tapped her chin and said, "Why, yes! I do believe we're still paying off the deductible on the broken window." I thought this was very uncharitable of her, considering the fact that we were talking about my attempted murder, so I turned to my father for support, but all he said was, "Are you sure you didn't do something to provoke the Filbender boy?"

"I did the right thing, if that's what you mean," I replied, with a meaningful look at Ruth, who gave me another hug.

In the end, my mother decided that the least I deserved was an apology from Lyle for the snowball to the face.

"Okay," said my father reluctantly. "I'll take him over first thing tomorrow morning and see what Lyle Senior has to say about all this."

●●●●●

Lyle Senior had plenty to say about all this, and none of it sympathetic toward me, I might add.

We walked to his place right after breakfast. I was feeling warm all over, and it had nothing to do with the steaming mug of cocoa I'd enjoyed alongside my six Eggo waffles and plateful of breakfast sausages. No, as we tromped up the steps of the Filbender residence, I was glowing with the knowledge of how humiliated Lyle was going to feel when he was forced to his knees to beg for my forgiveness.

You can imagine my surprise, then, when the front door flew open before we'd even rung the bell, and

 Tape #3

Mr. Filbender launched into a noisy harangue about how I'd ripped up the only copy of BISOB's petition.

"You told me you'd done nothing to provoke that boy!" exclaimed my father in dismay.

"No," I replied calmly. "I said I'd done the right thing."

Mr. Filbender exploded!

"How was that the right thing?" he shouted.

I tried to explain that if I hadn't ripped up the petition, Janine would have made me for a fraud and this would have irreparably damaged my reputation, but no one was listening. Mr. Filbender thrust a blank petition form into my father's unsuspecting hands, prattled on for a while about how he assumed that BISOB could count on him to gather replacement signatures for the petition I'd destroyed, then disappeared back into his lair as abruptly as he'd appeared.

When we got home, my mother asked how it had gone.

"There was no apology," I announced as I marched in and flopped down in front of the television. "Only more abuse, and Dad didn't even stick up for me." My mother followed my father into the kitchen to find out what had happened. A few minutes later, I heard them arguing about divided loyalties, and I must say that the sound of my mother sticking up for me for once in her life was almost as heartwarming as the sight of Lyle begging for my forgiveness would have been.

●●●●●

My grandmother called tonight and she was not at all pleased with me. Apparently, Mr. Filbender called to let her know about the shredded petition.

"Have you forgotten about six potatoes for eight hungry mouths?" she demanded in a voice quivering with emotion. "Have you forgotten about your promise?" When I pointed out that I'd only promised to *think* about the potato situation but hadn't actually committed myself on the soup kitchen question one way or another, I thought she'd have a stroke. After a few moments of ragged breathing, however, she managed to collect herself and gasp that while I was certainly causing her grief with my heartless mischief, she blamed my parents for not raising me right.

"Me, too," I said. "Maybe it's time for another visit — your personal involvement could be the very thing they need to shake off their cloak of complacency and start doing right by me." She said she'd think about it, and I hope that means yes. Her enormous spending power and tendency to undermine my parents have always been a great comfort to me.

•••••

I found BISOB's blank petition in the recycling bin this morning.

"You should put this somewhere safe," I advised, handing it back to my father. "Otherwise, you're going to lose it and what would everyone think of you then?" My father thanked me for the advice, but later I found the very same petition stuffed in the kitchen garbage under a soggy filter full of used coffee grounds.

I give up. If he doesn't care enough about his own reputation to run with the herd, it's not my problem.

•••••

A reporter and photographer from the *Winnipeg Gazette* newspaper showed up on our doorstep this evening. I was so excited! Apparently Ruth called to let them know how I'd been maimed for a good cause, and the editors thought it would be a terrific community interest story. The reporter — a fetching young thing in tortoiseshell glasses — asked me all sorts of questions about the incident and my involvement with the Mission. I answered as honestly as I could, taking pains to emphasize the fact that Lyle Filbender was a violent psychopath and that I'd given hardly any thought at all to the possibility of receiving a special award in recognition of my devotion to the cause. The reporter scratched notes with almost as much enthusiasm as my fine-looking psychologist, Dr. Anderson, used to, and afterward, the hippie photographer in the beaded vest took a close-up of me looking pale, pained and pitiful.

•••••

I made page two! Janine brought the paper to school and showed it around, and I must say, I looked devilishly handsome in spite of my pained expression and grievous injury. The article called me a shining example for all young people, and although Lyle Filbender wasn't mentioned by name, reference was made to a "known troublemaker," which I found just as satisfying. The only cloud in the sky of my happiness was John Michael, who refused to participate in the unbridled adulation of my starstruck classmates.

I wonder what his problem is.

•••••

I tried to ask Daryl what he thought John Michael's problem was, but instead of answering he asked me what my problem was.

"What are you talking about?" I asked. In response, he dug into the back of my pants in search of my underwear so that he could give me a good-natured atomic wedgie. When I confessed that I wasn't wearing any underwear because my old pair had disintegrated and my new pairs were too fresh to be comfortable, he hauled me up by the belt loop of my acid-wash jeans and marched me around his living room on tiptoe until I'd finished belting out all three verses of Yankee Doodle.

I guess he hasn't heard that I'm a shining example for all young people. Perhaps I'll stick a copy of my article in his mailbox.

•••••

Due to his inability to curb my behavior, my father has been temporarily suspended by the BISOB executive council. He was very upset when he heard the news, but I reminded him that I had suffered the indignity of probation status while working as a newspaper delivery boy. I assured him that these things sound worse than they are, and that if he bent to the will of his oppressors, he'd be back on top in no time.

If I weren't destined to rule a dynasty, I think I'd become a motivational speaker. I am as inspiring as it gets.

•••••

Horrible news! Horrendous, hideous, hair-raising news! My parents have cashed in my Christmas certificate entitling me to a crash course in traditional Ukrainian dance — I start in three days.

"You did this to get back at me because I ruined your reputation with BISOB!" I shouted at my father. When he denied it, I turned to my mother and shouted, "You did this to assuage your guilt about going back to work next week and making me a latchkey kid!"

"Don't be ridiculous," she replied. "I'm only working part-time — I'll be home most days before three o'clock. We did it because the certificate expires at the end of the month."

Utterly deflated, I wandered into the TV room to watch golf and contemplate my fate.

Later, I told my father that I would not soon forget his spitefulness or my mother's pending neglect.

"Yes you will, son," he said gently. "You have a very short attention span."

• • • • •

My mother brought home her breast-feeding demonstration gear, and it includes a plastic breast. It's not the most alluring breast in the world, because it's perched on a metal stick, but it's still a breast, so I've been gazing at it in secret whenever possible. I've even tried stroking it in order to practice my technique, but since it's cold, hard plastic, I don't think the skills I've developed are going to come in handy when I'm dating live women. Unless I'm dating women who've had breast implants, of course, in which case I think my technique will be right on the money.

• • • • •

John Michael came over after school, and after we finished eating the snack my mother laid out for us, we snuck into her bedroom so I could show him the breast-on-a-stick. He was impressed by the nipple detail, but agreed that the overall appeal was somewhat reduced by the 3-D cross section showing swollen milk ducts nestled in adipose tissue. Nevertheless, we took turns stroking it and comparing techniques, until John Michael suddenly asked, "Why'd you let the newspaper write that stuff about you being a shining example for young people? They made it sound like you're some kind of soup kitchen hero, and you're not even doing anything to help." Flustered, I said that things weren't always what they seemed and that it was unkind to judge a book by its cover.

"Let's not let politics tear our friendship apart," I added solemnly, before suggesting that we try one of my mother's bras on the breast and practice unhooking it with one hand. Thankfully, John Michael thought this sounded like fun and agreed to drop the uncomfortable subject of my self-serving behavior.

$$\bullet\ \bullet\ \bullet\ \bullet\ \bullet$$

I had my first dance class tonight. The instructor was a bona fide Ukrainian named Vlad Baryluk and he worked me to a state of near collapse. Vlad said that although spirit, fire and flexibility are important, fitness is the foundation of traditional Ukrainian dance. "And in the short time I have with you," he added, grinding a fist into the palm of his other hand, "I plan to whip you into the best physical shape of your young lives."

We fell into formation, and it was like something out of a nightmare. Run! Leap! Twist! Again! Eyes up! Arms down! Kick! Again! I was lined up next to a girl named Felicity, and she was an uncoordinated dolt who kept getting in the way of my flailing limbs. She said it was me who was uncoordinated, and also that I was short and unattractive. After class, I complained to Vlad about these thinly veiled insults, but he just grinned and said, "Sweat is tonic for the injured soul!" Next thing I knew, I was wobbling through a grueling set of ten half push-ups.

Vlad better back off pushing the benefits of sweat. Otherwise, I'm not going to learn to appreciate his art at all.

●●●●●

I gave myself a hickey with my mother's demonstration breast pump this evening. Now I'm going to have to fabricate a story about a vigorous make-out session with a mystery female, because hickeys are pretty cool, but not if you applied them yourself with the help of your mother's demonstration breast pump.

From now on, I'm going to stay away from her lactation paraphernalia. I like the plastic breast all right, but I knew that breast pump was going to be trouble the minute I applied it to my neck. If you ask me, those things should have a warning label.

●●●●●

I told the lads at school that I got hot and heavy with a chick in my dance class named Felicity. They snickered and joked and jostled one another for a closer look at my hickey, and before I knew it, rumors about Felicity and me were flying fast and furious.

In hindsight, I feel a bit bad that Felicity's name was dragged through the mud like that, but I have my own reputation to think about, after all, and no one's going to think of me as a stud if I don't brag about the occasional conquest. And anyway, I don't know for a fact that Felicity *isn't* the tramp the guys have painted her to be — for all I know, she may yet make good on the rumors they've been spreading!

The more I think about it, the more I realize that the real lesson here is that we shouldn't judge a person too harshly until the person who that first person has helped fuel rumors about shows her true colors.

• • • • •

I tried to be extra pleasant to Felicity during this evening's dance class. I searched her face carefully for signs that she might be thinking of compromising herself with me on account of my newfound pleasantness, but she is a very sly girl who hid her intentions well beneath a mask of being extremely irritated with me for hammering down on her feet repeatedly with my snappy new dance shoes. Afterward, as she hobbled off to get changed, I heard her referring to me as a "clod" and a "klutz" to the other girls.

A clod? A klutz? In addition to being sly, Felicity is also insensitive. Doesn't she know that a person's feelings can be injured by name-calling? Not to mention how embarrassing it is to be the subject of changing room gossip that isn't even true? I'm not a clod *or* a klutz, I'm just having difficulty getting used to my new shoes.

Boy. That Felicity deserves what she gets.

• • • • •

The rumors about Felicity and me have escalated dramatically in recent days, and the school is abuzz with talk of an impending sexual encounter between us. I've refused to comment on the gossip, but I've given myself several additional hickeys with my mother's demonstration breast pump, and it's clear that I've won untold amounts of respect from my fellow classmates. Except for the classmates that are girls, of course. Those classmates think I'm a pig.

• • • • •

Mr. Bennet pulled me aside today and said that he'd been hearing some disturbing rumors about me. I got very defensive.

"If this is about me being a klutz in dance class," I shouted, "it's a stinking, rotten lie!" When he clarified that it was actually about me becoming sexually active, I gave him a lecherous smile and several suggestive winks. He grimaced and said, "I hope you aren't forgetting all the important lessons we learned in Family Life, because I don't want to see anyone get hurt." I thanked him for his concern but told him not to worry.

"I know better than to get emotionally involved with a girl like Felicity," I said. "Besides, she's only interested in one thing, and I'm *not* talking about a committed relationship, if you know what I mean."

After a few more winks and a low, lewd chuckle, I sauntered off with my head held high. Mr. Bennet can interpret my comments any way he likes, but he can't ever say that I didn't tell him the truth. Because the fact is, I'm absolutely certain that Felicity *is* only interested in one thing: seeing me drop dead.

• • • • •

At Mr. Bennet's request, Dr. Anderson scheduled an impromptu session with me today in order to ask if I had any issues with women. I told her, "Not at all!" and said that I was a big fan of women unless they were aggressive or used their intelligence in a way that made men feel small. I laughed and said, "Can you blame me?" but she just scribbled some notes down in my file.

I hope Dr. Anderson didn't take any offense at my comments. While it's true that she's a little too intelligent, she's also very attractive, and that kind of cancels out the intelligence thing. Perhaps I should have clarified myself.

• • • • •

Of all the terrible coincidences — Felicity is Miss Thorvaldson's niece! Apparently, Miss Thorvaldson heard the rumors that have been going around, and since Felicity is a very uncommon name, and since she has a niece named Felicity who happens to be taking a traditional Ukrainian dance class, Miss Thorvaldson put two and two together and concluded that the Felicity people were talking about was the Felicity to whom she was related.

When she confronted me, I gave a low whistle and said, "You must have been disappointed when you learned what Felicity was up to," because I felt sure that things would go better for me if I were able to convince her that the gossip I'd started wasn't a complete fabrication. It obviously didn't work, however, because she's going to make me stand up in front of the class tomorrow and deny ever having had any physical contact with that sly tart Felicity. She was adamant about this, even after I revealed the embarrassing true origin of my hickeys and pointed out how ridiculous it would make me look in the eyes of my peers.

"Couldn't we leave the hickeys in and blame the rest of it on insensitive speculation by my filthy fellow guys?" I pleaded. "That way, we'd all win — my reputation would be preserved and people would still think of your niece as a fun girl, even if she doesn't go all the way." I smiled hopefully and said, "There's nothing wrong with having a reputation for being fun, is there?"

but I guess Miss Thorvaldson didn't see it that way. There must be something here that I'm missing.

• • • • •

I've learned a very important lesson from the whole Felicity incident, and that is that public retractions are very humiliating. And if guys can be quite unforgiving when you've played them for a bunch of chumps, girls are definitely worse. For some inexplicable reason, my female classmates continued to treat me like a pig, even after I came clean about the filthy rumors I'd helped fuel. Go figure! I pointed out to Missy Shoemaker that there was no reason to persist with this treatment, because I never actually took advantage of what's-her-name, but she just said, "Oink, oink," and asked if I had a date with my mother's vacuum cleaner this weekend. I laughed scornfully and explained that my mother has an upright vacuum cleaner, not a canister one, which makes it virtually impossible to apply a concentrated amount of suction to my skin.

What a fool Missy Shoemaker is! It is hard to believe that a female could know so little about vacuum cleaners.

• • • • •

Today when I got to dance class, Felicity stalked over and said, "I heard all about your disgusting rumors, and I'm going to ask Vlad to reassign me to a new place in the chorus line." Luckily, Vlad was unable to comply with her request, because none of the girls would volunteer to switch places with her. I was pleased that her unkind intentions toward me had been thwarted until about fifteen minutes later, when she caught me square in the belly with a spinning high kick that left me crumpled on the dance floor, gasping for breath. I used the incident as an excuse to loll on the sidelines protesting exhaustion and injury, but this turned out to be a terrible mistake, because after class, Vlad ordered me to join him and his advanced dance class for an early morning jog on Saturday.

"You are falling apart," he cried. "We need to do something before the finale!"

I told him he was dreaming and that my parents would never allow such a thing, but when my mother came to pick me up, she said, "What a terrific idea!" Hearing this, Vlad put down the garlic sausage and sauerkraut sandwich he'd been nibbling between classes, clamped his powerful hands firmly around my biceps and breathed inspiring words of camaraderie into my face until I threatened to pass out from the fumes.

●●●●●

As promised, Vlad showed up at my front door this morning with an entire troupe of limber youths in matching sweat suits.

"You can't be serious!" I protested, shivering in my Smurf pajamas. "It's twenty below out there!" In response, one of the youths fell backward onto his bare hands and started kicking his feet in the air, while the others clapped and shouted, "HI! HI! HI!" Snarling, I stomped upstairs, changed and joined them outside, where I started running as slowly as I possibly could. After a few minutes, I could tell that Vlad and the boys were getting itchy, so I panted, "You go ahead — I'll catch up. I promise!" Of course, I had no intention of catching up. My plan was to turn around and hurry back to bed the minute they were out of sight, but as

 Tape # 3

I rounded the corner at the top of the street, I came face-to-face with a mob!

There they were — Marv, Felix, Mr. Filbender, the other BISOB members — picketing the Holy Light Mission, while Jerry's gang shouted for them to stop blocking the door, because people needed to get through. I guess there had already been some shoving and name-calling, because the police were there and the media, too — snapping pictures and conducting interviews. It was exactly the kind of scene I wanted no part of, but as I turned to slink back into the shadows, I heard someone shout my name. Turning, I saw the young reporter with the tortoiseshell glasses running toward me.

"You're a big supporter of the soup kitchen," she cried, pushing a tape recorder in my face. "But we've recently learned that your family owns a local business and that your father is an active member of the BISOB organization. Are you going to cross the picket line — or are you going to support your family?"

It was a horrible moment made more horrible by the sight of the CTY television crew pulling up and spilling out of their van. I thought about the statements I'd made in my page-two article and how it would look if I retracted them now; I thought about how furious Marv and my grandmother would be if I *didn't* retract them. Then I looked up and saw Jerry staring at me through the grimy window of the Mission door. He looked so defeated that I suddenly didn't have the heart to turn my back on him — at least, not in front of all those people. Grumbling and clomping across the street in snowy sneakers, I slowly pushed my way through the picket line and into the Mission.

Pandemonium erupted. Outside, Marv pounded on

the Mission door and bellowed, "No more free Twinkies for you, pal!" Inside, Jerry was jubilant.

"Actions speak louder than words!" he cried, dancing around. I tried to explain that it didn't mean anything — that I'd acted in a moment of weakness — but my words were lost when Jerry's gang burst into a chorus of "Amazing Grace."

•••••

My parents and I watched me on the six o'clock news this evening. In spite of my earlier misgivings concerning the BISOB backlash, I have to admit it was a thrill to see the stalwart figure I cut as I trudged silently through the snow and into the Mission. Who knew a person could look that good in leg warmers?

After my segment was over, I asked my father why he hadn't been walking the picket line. He reminded me about his BISOB suspension. I thought about that for a moment, then asked, "So are you mad that I crossed the picket line?"

He looked at me strangely, then shook his head and gave me a hug.

•••••

Aunt Maud and Ruth just caught me on the late news. When they called to congratulate me, Ruth was so fired up that Aunt Maud could hardly get a word in edgewise.

"I just knew you'd develop a social conscience someday!" she gushed. "I knew all those rallies weren't wasted on you — that you'd figure out there's more to life than boiled wieners, TV reruns and looking out for Number One!" I told her to hold it right there — that there was no need to start trash-talking things that were

important to me — but she obviously thought I was joking because she started laughing like crazy. She said that seeing this kind of transformation in someone like me renewed her faith in humanity, and made her very, very proud, besides.

"Ditto, champ," said Aunt Maud, with a smile in her voice. "Keep up the good work."

•••••

When John Michael came to collect me for school this morning, he was grinning from ear to ear.

"I saw you on the news last night," he said. "You're right. I guess things aren't always what they seem." He was so pleased to discover that I wasn't a two-faced jerk that I didn't bother to correct him, and when we got to school and Janine ran up and threw her arms around me, I didn't bother to correct her, either (though I did put the squeeze on her). Everyone was impressed by my picket line escapade, except for Lyle Filbender and Theodore Pinker, who sat in a corner, whispering and glowering at me, and Missy Shoemaker, who flounced over and said I was about as genuine as a three dollar bill.

"That's a very unkind thing to say, Missy," I murmured, reaching for Janine's hand. "I ... I know I'm only one person, but I'm doing what I can."

Later, I asked Miss Thorvaldson if she'd seen me on the news, and she muttered that she had. I waited for her to shower me with compliments about my selfless behavior, but she just told me to get out of the staff room and leave her alone while she was trying to eat lunch.

•••••

We had the Ukrainian dance finale this evening. My performance would have been breathtaking if that troublemaker Felicity hadn't broken her toe under my heel during the second number. She went down like a sack of potatoes, embarrassing me in front of everybody. Then she got a three-minute standing ovation when she limped off the stage without assistance. I, on the other hand, got hardly any applause at all when I did an impromptu break-dancing routine in an attempt to draw attention back to me. I felt this was patently unfair. Traditional Ukrainian dance has its charms, but nothing compares to the Worm.

• • • • •

My grandmother called to say that all this nonsense about that dang soup kitchen has gone far enough and that she's coming to town to drag me back onto the straight-and-narrow before it's too late. I tried to calm her down by assuring her that deep down, no one was more keen to protect his own interests than I, but she snapped, "Deep down don't amount to a hill of beans." So then I said that if my recent antics had upset her so much, my feelings wouldn't be hurt if she decided to stay with my aunt Maud and Ruth instead of us.

"What would be the point of that?" she demanded. "I can't put my only grandson right if I'm not by his side, showing him the way these things are done! Besides," she continued, sounding a little petulant, "the very thought of Maud's *partner* gives me spasms! At least your father is a man, more or less." I told her he'd be pleased to hear that she felt that way. She hasn't always had such positive things to say about his masculinity, you know.

My parents, of course, are in a real state over the news of her pending arrival. My mother says that between starting a new job and trying to show equal

support to my father and me as we publicly do battle over the soup kitchen, she's got enough to worry about without her own mother showing up and making trouble. My father hasn't said anything specific, but whenever anybody mentions my grandmother's visit, he leans over and puts his head between his knees. I'm no expert in these matters, but I get the feeling that's not a good sign.

• • • • •

My grandmother arrived this evening. My parents and I went to the airport to pick her up, because my aunt Maud was in surgery and Ruth has been in a snit ever since I passed along the fact that the thought of her gives my grandmother spasms. Our reunion was very touching. My grandmother marveled at how wonderful we all looked — all except for my mother, who appeared tired and frumpy, and my father, who seemed to have shrunk. The pleasantries were short-lived, however, because my grandmother insisted on spending the entire drive home telling us all about the plans she has for winning the soup kitchen fight. These include encouraging the media to report on trouble caused by the Mission's unsavory fringe element and turning our dining room into a "War Room" in order to give the BISOB organization a permanent headquarters from which to work.

"And I'm expecting big things from you," she declared, stabbing a finger at my father as he single-handedly dragged her three gigantic steamer trunks up the front steps of our house. "Be forewarned that I shall consider these next weeks the ultimate test of your character."

"Me, too," he panted, collapsing in the front hall.

Well, at least they're on the same page. It's a start.

•••••

The *Winnipeg Gazette* has run two articles profiling several unpleasant-looking street people who spend their days harassing regular citizens or loitering in public before heading to the Mission for dinner. When, at my grandmother's behest, I called Jerry to tell him that I was having second thoughts about supporting such a degenerate bunch, he protested that most of the Mission's clients weren't street people at all, and that many of those who were suffered from mental illnesses and therefore couldn't be held responsible for the sad state of their own affairs. I was so surprised by this information that after I got off the phone with Jerry, I decided to call the reporter with the tortoiseshell glasses and share it with her.

"That's interesting," she said. "But I'm afraid it's not the angle we're taking with this story." When I tried to ask what angles had to do with facts, she said she had to go.

•••••

Ruth has been leaving inspirational messages for me on our answering machine. Mostly, they have to do with walking the road less traveled and not faltering when horrible, mean-spirited, close-minded ugly ogres descend upon me in the hopes of breaking my spirit and luring me from the path of social justice.

"I know she gives you spasms," I told my grandmother this afternoon as I played back yet another message. "But doesn't she just have a way with words?" In response, my grandmother made a sound like she was coughing up a fur ball and sailed out of the room.

• • • • •

There was another article in the *Winnipeg Gazette* today — this time, profiling several well-respected local businessmen who have nothing at all against the Mission but who care so deeply about keeping the community safe for decent citizens that they feel compelled to support its closure. Mr. Bennet cut the article out of the paper and we discussed it in Family Life class. Hardly any of my classmates were fooled by the way it tried to make the businessmen seem like heroes. Janine pointed out that people don't eat at a soup kitchen unless they have no other option.

"And if they have no other option," she said, "what are they going to do if it gets shut down?" John Michael added that we'd be surprised who eats at a place like the Mission — that they're mostly regular people like the rest of us. When he said this, Lyle Filbender rolled his eyes and asked Mr. Bennet what a soup kitchen had to do with Family Life, anyway.

"Lots, I suppose, if it's where your family eats dinner," he replied.

Then Missy Shoemaker — whose dad works as a senior city bureaucrat — piped up and said that our discussion was all fine and well, but the fact was that things weren't looking good for the Mission. Apparently, her dad heard through the grapevine that the petitions came in and there were a lot more signatures in support of closing it than against.

"The articles in the newspaper haven't helped, either," she said importantly. "And the mayor's concerned about how giving money to a place like that might affect his image in an election year."

This really got everyone going — everyone but me, that is. My grandmother has been indulging my every whim from the moment she stepped off the plane. It only seems right that I repay her by keeping my mouth shut.

• • • • •

This evening, after gulping down half a bottle of Maalox to protect her delicate digestive system from the assault of my mother's cooking, my grandmother conducted her first BISOB meeting as honorary chairwoman. It was a historic occasion marked by a prolonged standing ovation at the conclusion of her opening address, followed by a good deal of griping over the public relations backlash inspired by that last *Gazette* article. Seems like a number of decent citizens weren't fooled by the way it tried to make the businessmen sound like heroes, either, and today's letters to the editor had some pretty scathing things to say about BISOB. My grandmother had to bang our dining room table with a heavy wooden mallet many times before she was able to restore order and turn the floor over to my father, whom she'd tasked with digging up more dirt on Jerry and his gang. Much to her chagrin, however, he hadn't found a single thing, and the meeting broke up a short while later.

After everyone left, my grandmother was eager to find out if the evening had appropriately influenced my cockamamie views on the place of soup kitchens in the world of business, but my mother said it was late and I had to go to bed. When my grandmother protested that it was inhumane to send a boy my age to bed without a decent snack and handed me another giant slice of the chocolate cake she'd let me gorge myself on before dinner, my mother flatly refused to allow me to eat it, and even sounded a little cranky when my grandmother questioned her judgment.

Although I'm not usually one to interfere, I may have to mention something to my mother about her intractable attitude. My grandmother obviously has a lot of wisdom she could share if only my mother would stop being so defensive about it.

• • • • •

I mentioned to my mother about her attitude problem and she didn't take it well at all. She told me it was a rude, intrusive comment, gave me a long, boring lecture about *my* attitude problem and lack of loyalty and finished up by saying that I had no idea what it was like trying to deal with a woman as hardheaded and difficult as my grandmother. When I gave her a meaningful look and said, "Oh, I think I have an idea," she pinched her lips together and sent me to my room.

Boy, you'd think my mother would've appreciated the hint that she's turning into her mother instead of acting so snippy about it. She must be further gone than I thought.

• • • • •

Since the majority of the class is in favor of saving the Holy Light Mission, Mr. Bennet has proposed that we do a twenty-four-hour famine to raise money and show our support. "It could be a good way to bring attention to the plight of people who depend on that soup kitchen to fill their stomachs," he said.

Quaking in my boots, I asked, "What exactly do you mean by a twenty-four-hour famine?"

Mr. Bennet explained that we wouldn't eat anything for twenty-four hours.

"What exactly do you mean by anything?" I cried, quaking even harder.

"By anything, I mean anything," he smiled. "You'll be able to drink as much water as you want, but that's it. What do you think?"

I thought it sounded even more inhumane than my mother not allowing me to eat chocolate cake before bed, but before I could propose any reasonable arguments opposing this insanity, Missy Shoemaker grinned at me and said, "I think it's a terrific idea! Don't you?" I was nearly blinded by the sudden urge to snap her bra as a punishment for putting me on the spot, but I could see Janine and John Michael both looking at me expectantly, so I peeled my lips back in a grotesque parody of a smile and croaked, "You bet I do!"

We spent the rest of the class making plans. Mr. Bennet said he'd get permission for us to stay overnight in the gym; Janine said she'd notify Jerry; Missy Shoemaker said she'd draw up the pledge sheets. I gloomily offered to contact the media. Only Lyle Filbender and Theodore Pinker refused to participate, and I can't say it was much of a loss.

• • • • •

I called Mr. Fitzgerald, my ex-overlord at the *Winnipeg Daily News*, to let him know about the twenty-four-hour famine and to offer him a nonexclusive paid interview. He didn't seem very appreciative of my kind offer — in fact, he sounded downright annoyed.

"How'd you get my private number?" he demanded.

"Easy!" I replied. "I told your assistant it was an emergency."

He muttered something about putting her on probation — big surprise! — then told me that he was categorically uninterested in an interview, paid or otherwise.

I was hurt, but resolved to sign off on a high note by asking Mr. Fitzgerald if the little honey who'd answered the phone was his first wife. When he made a strangled sound and said, "That was my daughter!" I asked how old she was and if she was seeing anybody. I explained that I was currently in the market for a new romantic entanglement because my last encounter had ended badly when some false rumors I'd accidentally started destroyed the girl's reputation. I assured him that the experience had taught me a lesson, however, and that now I don't bother with girls who are so wrapped up in what other people think of them.

"Is your daughter one of those girls?" I asked.

He didn't answer, except to say that I was never to call his house again.

"That's going to make things difficult if I start dating your daughter," I warned, but he hung up without even saying good-bye.

Mr. Fitzgerald obviously has no idea how to treat his sources. After the excellent scoop I gave him, the least he could have done was put in a good word for me with his daughter.

• • • • •

I left a message for the beautiful Lori Anderson of CTY television, chastising her for not giving me any coverage at Christmas when I was being persecuted by Miss Thorvaldson, giving her lukewarm credit for televising my dramatic picket line crossing and encouraging her to stop by the school next Monday night to catch a local hero starving himself for the cause. If that doesn't get her attention, I don't know what will.

• • • • •

My grandmother has refused to give me pledge money in support of my twenty-four-hour famine.

"I don't like it any more than you do," I grumbled. "But for the sake of my reputation, I'm pretending to like it. Can't you pretend to respect my conviction?"

"No," she said, stalking out of the room in search of my mother — and a warm cup of tea, if that wouldn't be too much to ask.

Later, when Ruth and Aunt Maud stopped by for a short, uncomfortable visit with my grandmother, I told them about the famine. Aunt Maud warned me to stay hydrated and avoid strenuous physical activity, and pledged ten dollars. Ruth looked so pleased and proud that I almost felt embarrassed. She was about to pledge twenty dollars when my grandmother rolled her eyes and gave a disapproving sniff. Cocking her head to one side, Ruth said, "On second thought — this is such a worthwhile cause, let's make it forty!" I wondered if my grandmother would sniff again and up the ante, but she just folded her arms tightly across her chest, pinched her lips together and looked away.

• • • • •

I've decided to chronicle what could very well be the final twenty-four hours of my life. I can't believe I got roped into this stinking famine! My stomach's grumbling already — though it's possible that this is a result of the jumbo bag of Fudgee-Os I wolfed down in the car on the way over. It was a last, desperate effort to stave

off the terrible effects of starvation, and it's starting to give me cramps. I'd better go find a place to unroll my sleeping bag ... while I'm still able.

●●●●●

Feeling weak! Disoriented! Dizzy! Must ... ask ... Mr. Bennet ... for ... sustenance ...

●●●●●

I asked Mr. Bennet for sustenance and instead of slipping me a dollar for the vending machine, he called everyone to gather around and sing songs of inspiration. Then he pointed out that we'd only been here for half an hour and sent me to the supply room for the floor mats.

●●●●●

For the last three hours, we've been playing board games in a feeble attempt to distract ourselves from the hunger that threatens to consume us all. Well, that threatens to consume me, anyway. I wound up in a game of Monopoly with Missy Shoemaker and spent three consecutive turns in jail before eventually landing at the hotel on her Boardwalk property and being bankrupted. I pointed out that this officially made me a poor person and suggested that she show me a little of the compassion that had inspired her to be such a monumental pain in the neck about this twenty-four-hour famine business, but she just cackled and flicked my top hat into oblivion.

●●●●●

As we were getting ready for bed, Jerry dropped by with some terrific news. Tomorrow night — precisely twenty-four hours after this madness began — we're all invited to break our fast at the Holy Light Mission, where the beautiful Lori Anderson of CTY television will be waiting to interview us. I gave a weak, "Hurrah!" and was preparing to lower myself back into the fetal position, when Janine — who was bouncing around in a pair of oversized pink flannel pajamas — threw her teddy bear to one side and gave me a rapturous hug that seemed to last forever. Afterward, I tottered over to Mr. Bennet and panted, "I'm definitely feeling disoriented and dizzy now!" He just smiled and told me to put my head between my knees.

•••••

A few minutes ago, Mr. Bennet caught me rummaging around in the refrigerator in the staff room. I'd waited patiently until I thought everyone was asleep, then snuck out of the gym to scavenge the school for anything edible. I initially thought the staff room fridge was empty, but then I spied a mangled sandwich that had fallen behind one of the crispers. I dug it out and was just about to take a bite when the beam of a flashlight hit me. Thinking fast, I stuck my arms straight out in front of me and moaned, "I ... must ... be ... sleepwalking." Gullible old Mr. Bennet murmured, "My goodness!" pried the moldy sandwich out of my clutching hand and gently guided me back to the gym without attempting to wake me.

•••••

Dawn broke on a pitiful sight: two dozen hungry adolescents sipping chilled Evian water instead of pigging out on Lucky Charms and breakfast sausages. I have now witnessed true hardship.

•••••

The day has passed in a haze. Several times, Miss Thorvaldson found me staggering through the halls, but instead of inquiring after my dangerously low blood sugar, she reprimanded me for taking the bathroom pass and disappearing for half an hour. I tried to explain about the hallucinations that often occur as the body begins to consume its own tissues, but she just snapped, "Get your arm out of that vending machine and get back to class this minute!" I did, but I lurched and muttered to myself the whole way in order to prove that I wasn't faking about those hallucinations.

•••••

They say that no good deed goes unpunished, and that goes double for anything involving that good-for-nothing Jerry.

As planned, we showed up at the soup kitchen at the stroke of six o'clock. I was so overcome by the prospect of eating again that I dropped to my knees and very nearly wept with joy. Then I scrambled to my feet and pushed my way to the front of the line because I was sure that Jerry would have ordered in the finest takeout as a show of gratitude, and I didn't want to miss out on one glorious bite.

Imagine my shock, then, when he slopped a bowl full of watery stew onto my orange plastic tray and ordered me down the line for my crust of stale bread and bruised apple.

"Are you kidding me?" I exclaimed. "I haven't eaten for twenty-four hours!" I think I would have had a full-blown temper tantrum if I hadn't noticed the beautiful

Lori Anderson ordering her television crew to zoom in on me. Giving a good-natured chuckle, I swallowed hard and thanked Jerry for his hospitality.

"Not at all," he replied warmly. "I'm just sorry we couldn't provide you with something more substantial." Then he turned to Lori Anderson and the television camera and explained that although it didn't seem like much, it was all some people would get between now and breakfast tomorrow morning. "The twenty-four-hour famine was a wonderful gesture, but to truly understand the plight of our clientele, these children would have to go to sleep on a bellyful of this food," said Jerry, motioning to my tray, "and return tomorrow morning for whatever meager breakfast we're able to provide. Because *that* is the reality of being too poor to feed yourself."

Lori nodded compassionately and then, with a toss of her honey blond curls, turned to us and said, "What about it kids? Are you up to the challenge?"

I would have vomited if I'd had anything in my stomach. I knew that rising to this insane challenge was exactly the kind of thing that goody-two-shoes Missy Shoemaker would do, and I couldn't let her get the better of me on television. I just couldn't! So, before she had a chance to open her big mouth and say something noble, I blurted, "Count me in, Lori!"

"Not me," declared Missy, a fraction of a second later. "I'm sorry, Ms. Anderson, but I'm *really* hungry, and after we eat here, Mr. Bennet said he'd take us all to Totally Fried Chicken for a celebration dinner."

The rest of my classmates mumbled and nodded in agreement. I almost collapsed. Lori Anderson laughed.

"Well, I don't blame you one bit," she admitted. "I

didn't actually expect anyone to take me up on my challenge. But since you have" — she smiled at me — "my camera crew and I will meet you here bright and early tomorrow morning to see how you've done."

After forcing down the barely edible contents of my tray, I dragged my shell-shocked carcass home to find my parents and grandmother watching a clip of my nightmare on the evening news. I quickly explained that it was a misunderstanding of astronomical proportions and that if I didn't eat real food soon I'd shrivel up and blow away in the wind, and I think my parents were on the brink of caving in when my grandmother stuck her formidable nose into the middle of it.

"The boy made a promise," she boomed, pointing at me so hard that she nearly gouged out my eye with her fingernail. "What's more, he had bread, soup and fruit for dinner, which is nothing to sneeze at. What possible harm could come of teaching him to keep his promises?"

We all knew she was just being spiteful because of all the good press I'd brought the Mission, but my mother sighed, "I hate to admit it, Mother, but I think you're right." Not believing my ears, I turned to my father, only to have him shrug. "She's got a point, son."

The world's gone mad.

• • • • •

It's half-past midnight and I just discovered my grandmother lying on an air mattress on the kitchen floor, guarding over the refrigerator. Her face was slathered with blue night cream, her hair was in a hairnet and her long, bony feet stuck out the end of a filmy, flowing white nightdress.

"I'm just trying to help you keep your promise," she

declared, putting the cucumber slices back onto her eyes.

She has no idea how effective her strategy was. There is a very good chance my appetite will never return.

•••••

This morning, after checking to make sure that last night's encounter with my grandmother hadn't turned my hair completely white, I slapped a handful of Dippity-do styling gel into my hair and hurried up to the Holy Light Mission for a well-deserved breakfast and a little personal attention from the one and only Lori Anderson. When I got there, however, Lori was nowhere to be seen.

"Where's the television crew?" I asked Jerry, looking around.

"Lori called a few minutes ago to say they wouldn't be able to make it," he replied. "I'm sorry — I guess you prolonged your suffering for nothing more than a chance to see how the other guy lives. Eggs?" He smiled, holding a plateful of scrambled eggs out to me.

Grumbling, I took it from him, but as I started to complain that it wasn't accompanied by crisp bacon and lightly buttered white toast, I noticed a familiar figure hunched over a similar plate at the far end of a nearby table.

It was Daryl!

It was weird seeing him there — I couldn't figure it out. But I know an opportunity when I see one, so I snuck up behind him and shouted, "BOO!"

The look on his face! Priceless!

"What are you doing here?" I asked, sitting down beside him. "I'm here because, like a fool, I agreed to eat two consecutive meals here with nothing decent in between." I used my fork to drag my soggy eggs around my plate. "Ugh. Would you look at this sludge?" I said, emptying a bottle of ketchup onto the egg pile. "And can you believe they have no sugar cereals in the bin? I mean, come on — do they honestly think anyone likes Shredded Wheat?" I chattered, shoveling the eggs into my mouth. "Was your school doing a twenty-four-hour famine, too?" I asked. "Is that why you're here?"

Strangely, Daryl didn't say one word during the whole meal, not even hello to the kitchen woman who walked by and said, "Good morning, Daryl."

"Are you sick?" I finally asked, licking my egg platter clean. "Because, you know, you didn't even try to hammer me when I yelled 'boo' at you." I gave him a poke in the side when I said this — hoping for a reaction — but he picked up his tray without looking at me and walked away.

•••••

While we were hanging around the boot scrapers waiting for the bell, I mentioned to John Michael about seeing Daryl at the Mission. He didn't say anything at first, but I could tell by the look on his face that he knew something, so I bugged him and bugged him until he reluctantly confided that Daryl sometimes eats breakfast there.

"What?" I gaped. *"Why?"*

John Michael looked around uncomfortably before leaning over and whispering, "Because otherwise, he goes to school hungry."

Goes to school hungry! I'm in shock. Could this really be true? I will have to follow up with Daryl.

•••••

I ran to Daryl's house after school today to find out the truth. At first, he just stared at the ceiling and said he didn't know what I was talking about.

"I'm talking about you eating breakfast at the soup kitchen, Daryl," I said, feeling bewildered. "I know this morning had nothing to do with a twenty-four-hour famine. John Michael told me that for you it was the real thing."

The next thing I knew, Daryl had tackled me into the wall. It wasn't a friendly, boisterous tackle meant to knock the wind out of me in a good-natured way — it was a real tackle, meant to hurt me. I was so stunned that I didn't even throw up my arms to block his punch. His fist connected with my face.

Daryl fell back at the sight of blood pouring from my nose. "Crap!" he muttered, scrambling for something to hold over my nose. When I refused the small, crumpled article of mystery clothing he'd picked off the floor, he ran to the bathroom for a wad of toilet paper. As he did so, I pinched my nose and wandered into the kitchen. That lone can of artichoke hearts I'd seen in his cupboard that time suddenly took on a whole new meaning.

"Here," he said, appearing abruptly and pushing the tissue toward me. We sat in silence, waiting for the bleeding to stop.

"I'm sorry, Daryl," I said eventually, cautiously checking my nose. "I didn't mean to make you angry."

"Well ... I'm sorry for hitting you," he said, gritting his teeth. "It's just that ... the whole soup kitchen thing is no big deal. I hardly ever go there. Honest."

"But you *sometimes* go there!" I exclaimed. "I feel just awful knowing you'd to go to school hungry otherwise."

"Still," he insisted. "It's no big deal, and you can't say anything to anybody about it, okay?"

Hand on heart, I promised that his secret was safe with me.

●●●●●

My mother was very upset when she saw the state of my nose.

"Did those Junior BISOB thugs do this to you?" she demanded.

"I don't want to talk about it," I replied in a voice that clearly blamed those Junior BISOB thugs but said I was too big a person to get dragged down to their level. She fretted about my stoic attitude for a while, then made such a production of my physical injuries — fetching an ice pack, checking for other lumps and abrasions, testing my pupil dilation — that I finally had to shoo her away.

"Quit fussing over me!" I cried, hopping down from the bathroom counter. "Honestly! What is wrong with you? There are kids out there with bigger problems than a bump on the nose, you know."

For some reason, saying this led her to believe that I might have suffered a slight concussion in the attack. I told her I'd never felt more clearheaded in my life, but she insisted on checking up on me every twenty minutes for the rest of the night.

●●●●●

I bolted out of bed this morning, got dressed and was waiting in front of the Mission when Jerry unlocked the door at seven o'clock.

"Jerry!" I shouted, startling him so badly that he spilled coffee down the front of his sweatshirt. "Do you realize there are kids who will go to school hungry if your Mission shuts down? Real live kids, Jerry! What are we going to do?"

Jerry didn't seem at all shocked by the news — perhaps he's worked with the poor for so long that he's grown immune to their suffering. Instead, he wondered if I had a fever and suggested that I sit down and rest awhile. I was thoroughly disgusted by the suggestion.

"Rest? There's no time to rest!" I cried. "We've got to do something!" In response, he tried to take my pulse, but I shook him off and hurried back home for a quick bite of breakfast before school.

●●●●●

After polishing off six slices of French toast, three glasses of orange juice, two blueberry muffins and a banana, I gave my mother a big hug and thanked her for doing her best — day in, day out — to put good, nourishing food on the table.

"It's not always appetizing," I admitted, giving her a final squeeze. "But it's almost always edible, and that's the important thing."

"Oh, stop," she said, flapping her hand at me. "You are too, too kind."

●●●●●

The minute I sat down at my desk this morning, I asked Missy Shoemaker if she would ask her father if there were any laws that would prohibit the Save Our Soup Kitchen movement from staging a sit-in down at City Hall.

"Hoping for a few more glamour shots with Lori Anderson, are you?" she sneered.

"No, of course not," I replied. "You said yourself that the fate of the Mission wasn't looking good. Maybe the twenty-four-hour famine helped, but we need to do more! There are kids out there who will go to school hungry if the Mission closes, you know." I waited for Missy to say something, but she just stared at me. "What?" I asked. Then I noticed that they were all staring me — John Michael, Theodore Pinker, Lyle Filbender — even Miss Thorvaldson. "What?" I repeated. "Why are you all looking at me that way? Do I have something hanging out of my nose?" I asked for the bathroom pass to go check for nasal debris and when I returned, class had begun.

• • • • •

My mother went grocery shopping today, so after she put everything away and went upstairs to run herself a well-deserved bubble bath, I emptied the fridge and the cupboards and hauled two grocery bags full of food to Daryl's house.

"What's all this?" he demanded, eyeing my grocery bags suspiciously.

"Milk, Daryl," I explained breathlessly. "And some sandwich meat. Fruit and fresh bread. Can I come in?"

"No!" he shouted, slamming the door in my face.

"But Daryl," I cried through the closed door. "I brought Lucky Charms. They're magically delicious!"

After a moment, the door opened a crack. "I've never had Lucky Charms," muttered Daryl.

"They're terrific!" I enthused, barging inside before he could slam the door in my face again.

I hauled the groceries into his kitchen and then, even though it wasn't breakfast time, we sat down on his stinky couch and ate bowlful after bowlful of Lucky Charms.

"Aren't they delicious?" I asked, partially chewed cereal spilling out of my full-to-bursting mouth.

"Magically," he replied, accidentally spraying me with a squirt of milk. He laughed as the milk dribbled down my face, so I loaded my spoon with a green clover and a couple of yellow moons and flicked it at him. I missed, but he evidently felt that my attempt deserved retaliation, because without warning he dumped the last of his cereal over my head and started jumping up and down on the couch with all his might. I bounced helplessly among the clouds of dust mites for quite some time, pleading for mercy, until he suddenly gave an ear-splitting Tarzan call and performed a drop jump that would have decapitated me if his elbow had landed in the right place.

"You're okay," he panted, giving me a slap on the back.

"So are you," I replied, getting up to rinse the milk off my head.

Later, my mother asked where all the groceries had gone.

"Beats me," I shrugged.

Daryl's secret is definitely safe with me.

● ● ● ● ●

This morning my father discovered that my grandmother has been shaving her armpits with his brand-new razor.

"Quit complaining!" I barked. "You don't know how good you have it!" I told him that his problems were nothing compared to the everyday struggle for survival that some people face and that he should be ashamed of himself for spearheading efforts to keep food out of

the mouths of hungry children. My grandmother evidently overheard my tirade, because she confronted me the minute I stalked out of the bathroom.

"You're ... you're being *ridiculous*," she spluttered. "What do you know about hungry children? God willing, I've forgotten more than you'll ever know on the subject and I'm telling you, one soup kitchen more or less isn't going to make a bit of difference! Why can't you just let it alone and help us take care of what's ours?"

I wanted to make her see — to make her *understand* — but before I could say anything, she jerked forward and clutched me in a brief, awkward embrace before hastily stepping back and fussing over the Dippity-do smear I'd left on the front of her dress. I didn't know what to say then, and I don't think she did, either. So, after a moment of embarrassed silence, we continued on our separate ways.

•••••

Missy Shoemaker's father believes that a sit-in down at city hall is exactly the wrong way to go.

"He says it would make us look militant," she explained.

I frowned and asked, "Well, does he have any suggestions?"

Missy eyed me suspiciously before nodding slowly. "He says that the city is in the middle of its annual budgetary process and that future funding for programs like Jerry's is being reviewed as a part of it. He thinks that speaking at the next city council meeting could be our best chance to directly influence the city councilors before they finalize funding decisions and vote on the budget."

I mulled this over. "Okay," I said at last. "I think your idea makes sense. I'll talk to Jerry about it after school and see what he thinks."

Missy gave me an uncertain smile and wandered off shaking her head.

•••••

Jerry signed us up!

The Holy Light Mission is fourth on the agenda at the next city council meeting, right after a group pushing the need for a new city cat shelter, the issue of bilingual parking tickets and the Save Our Green Space zealots, who oppose cutting down four trees in the Exchange District in order to accommodate a multimillion-dollar movie production company. Because the council has so much to get through that day, they've limited each side to two speakers, plus a rebuttal speaker.

As soon as I heard the news, I called Daryl and told him we were one step closer to saving the soup kitchen.

"Yeah?" he said. "Well, when you're done saving that, I think you should try saving Uranus."

I thanked him for the vote of confidence, but said that interplanetary rescue operations were just a little out of my league.

Later, after we hung up, I made a mental note to start following the news more closely. I didn't even realize Uranus was in trouble.

•••••

This evening, a bunch of us got together to talk strategy for the city council meeting.

"They need to know this means real food in the mouths of real people. People like me," I said, gesturing to myself.

"People like her," I said, resting my hands on the shoulders of the exotic dancer Honey, who was wearing a pink angora sweater that fit like a tube sock. Then I didn't say anything, because suddenly, I couldn't think of anything but how fluffy that angora felt between my fingers. I stood there in tongue-tied silence until Jerry walked over, pried my hands off Honey's shoulders and nominated me to be one of the speakers at the council meeting. John Michael seconded the motion, Janine clapped her hands and wriggled with excitement, and before I knew it, a vote was taken and the motion carried with flying colors. Much congratulating and glad-handing followed, and it wasn't until the meeting started to break up that I was able to pull Jerry aside and confess to him about my pathological fear of public speaking.

"You know me, Jerry," I whispered. "I'd do anything for the cause. I've been maimed for the cause! But please, please! Don't ask me to do this." Jerry seemed very surprised by the fact that I was a nervous public speaker. "Don't be fooled by my easy charm and happy-go-lucky attitude," I told him. "Even someone like me has something he's not good at."

Given that Jerry is a church person who's already pressed his luck with me on more than one occasion, I expected him to show mercy and let me off the hook this time. Fat chance! Instead of running with my suggestion — that he tell everyone I'm under a performance contract with NBC that prevents me from accepting public speaking engagements of any kind — Jerry led the room in another round of applause for the local hero who was as steadfast and brave as he was goodlooking.

"Just remember," he whispered as I was leaving. "That which doesn't kill us makes us stronger."

"Or else leaves us permanently traumatized," I hissed, stomping out into the cold.

•••••

I told my parents and grandmother that I'd been selected as a speaker for the Save Our Soup Kitchen side. I expected my grandmother to be furious about it, but instead, she said, "You?"

I was completely taken aback by her tone of disbelief. "Yes, me," I said. When she didn't say anything else, I added, "I'll have you know that I'm a gifted speaker." She hummed and tugged at a thread on the hem of her violet caftan until my mother suddenly exploded.

"Stop your humming and tugging!" she cried. "I always hated when you did little things like that to chip away at my self-confidence, and you will not do them to my son!" She turned to me. "Honey, I am very proud of you for having the courage to march up to that podium alone and speak your mind in front of all those hundreds of people. I just know you're going to do a wonderful job!" She threw her arms around me, and so did my father.

"Me too, son," he said gruffly. "Me too."

We embraced in loving silence, ignoring my grandmother, who glared at us like a sour purple grape. It was almost enough to keep the panic from sweeping through my veins like a malignant tide, engulfing every helpless cell in my body.

Almost.

•••••

Tonight before bed, I told my father how much it meant to me to know that I had his support and how pleased I was to see him finally throwing his weight behind

the Save Our Soup Kitchen campaign.

"I know grandmother's approval means a lot to you and that you badly want to be accepted by your fellow business owners," I said. "But I guess we've both come to realize that sometimes we have to make sacrifices for the things we believe in. As a grown-up, you probably should have figured this out long before me, but even so, I want you to know that I'm just as proud of you as I can be." He looked stunned and tried to stammer out a reply, but I cut him off with a hug that took his breath away.

•••••

Janine told Mr. Bennet that I'd been selected as a speaker for the city council meeting.

"What a coincidence," snarled Lyle Filbender. "As president of the Junior BISOB organization, I'm going to be speaking for the other side."

Mr. Bennet thought this was terrific news. "What a wonderful learning opportunity!" he enthused. "We'll split into teams, prepare arguments and debate the issue over and over. It'll be good practice for the real thing."

At that point, I started to feel so woozy that I had to put my head down on the desk.

"Are you okay?" asked Mr. Bennet. I nodded weakly, but later I privately explained that the last thing in the world I wanted was additional opportunities to speak in front of people. "Don't worry," he said. "I'll be right beside you every step of the way."

"Really?" I asked hopefully. "Even when I'm giving my speech at the city council meeting?"

"Well, no," admitted Mr. Bennet. "At the council meeting, I'm afraid you'll be on your own."

•••••

All is not lost! Mr. Bennet has revealed to me a time-honored technique designed to help nervous public speakers overcome their fear of the audience.

"Before you start speaking," he said, "look out over the crowd and imagine them sitting there in their underwear."

For a long, silent moment, I stood at the front of the class and did as he asked.

"There now," he said. "Don't you feel calmer?"

"Not exactly calmer," I said, grinning down at Missy Shoemaker, who scowled and crossed her arms over her chest. "But definitely better."

• • • • •

I've been practicing my new public speaking technique wherever possible — at the mall, in the grocery store, with Trish, the school secretary. It was going well until tonight at dinner, when I accidentally practiced it on my grandmother and nearly went blind at the sudden vision of her eating Baloney Noodle Surprise in her girdle.

"What's wrong?" cried my father, chasing after me as I shielded my eyes with my forearm and staggered from the room, screaming.

"Trust me," I gasped, collapsing into his arms. "You don't want to know."

• • • • •

My grandmother called an emergency BISOB meeting in her War Room this evening and barred me from attending on the grounds that I am a subversive.

"Fine with me," I retorted. "I've got to put the finishing touches on my brilliant city council speech, anyway." She gasped at my cheekiness and we stood staring at each other — hands on hips, chins thrust forward —

until she turned sharply, swept into the War Room and slammed the door behind her. I ran upstairs and pressed my ear to the floor vent just in time to hear her nominate my father for vice president of BISOB Media Relations. I smiled and waited for her reaction when my father told her to go jump in the lake, but it never came. Because instead of confessing that he had switched allegiances, my father just sat there and let them pass the motion!

I was on my feet and down the stairs in an instant, but my mother intercepted me before I could burst into the War Room and berate my father for being a traitor. She took me into the kitchen and made me wait quietly until the meeting broke up and everyone left, then sent my father in to talk to me.

To my immense satisfaction, he looked miserable. I spun around and faced the other direction the minute he sat down at the kitchen table.

"Son, try to understand," he pleaded, addressing the back of my head. "I didn't mean to mislead you — I just didn't know how to tell you. When you're an adult, things can be complicated. I've waited fourteen years for the opportunity to prove to your grandmother that your mother didn't marry beneath her. At this point, the funding decision for the Holy Light Mission could go either way. Turning my back on BISOB now would be a public relations disaster for them and could tip the balance. If it did — and if the House of Toilets suffered as a result — your grandmother would never forgive me. Or respect me. And I'd never be able to mend the rift in our family." He shook his head in frustration. "Believe it or not, I *am* thinking of our family, and when you stand up in front of city council, no one will be rooting harder for you than I."

I was quiet for just long enough to let him think that I was considering his point of view. Then I let him have it.

"That is the lamest speech I have ever heard," I said. "And I want you to know that in my entire life, I've never been so disappointed in you." He started to protest but I held up my hand. "You've made your position perfectly clear, so let me do the same: From now on, you are the enemy. And until this thing is over, I have nothing to say to you."

With that, I got up and marched out of the room. I thought he might try to follow, but he didn't. Later, I could hear him and my mother talking in the other room, but try as I might, I couldn't hear what they were saying.

•••••

I told John Michael and Daryl about my father's decision to stick with BISOB.

"He gave me a lot of excuses, but that's all they were — excuses," I said. "As far as I'm concerned, the gloves are off. Imagine being so self-centered that you can't see the bigger picture!" We all agreed that he was a jerk and that if adults ever bothered to take the advice that they so love to dump on us — do unto others and love thy neighbor and all that jazz — the world would be a better place by far.

•••••

My father has tried to speak to me several times, but on each occasion I have rebuffed him. When my mother tried to intercede on his behalf, she only made it worse by telling me that my father is a good man who wants nothing more than to see the soup kitchen stay open but who is grappling with what he sees as conflicting objectives.

"You mean he doesn't even want to see the Mission shut down?" I shouted. "He knows that what BISOB is doing is wrong and he's going along with it anyway?" I told her I'd remember that the next time someone offered me a hit of crack cocaine.

"Who offered you crack cocaine?" she asked in alarm.

"Oh, just some people I've been wanting to impress for a long time," I said breezily. "There's been this rift between the good kids and the drug addicts. It's hard to explain — these things can be *so* complicated." When she told me she didn't appreciate my sarcasm, I replied that I didn't appreciate my father's hypocrisy. "Or the way you're making excuses for him," I added. She didn't have anything to say to that.

•••••

My grandmother has been wandering around the house like a well-fed ghost these past few days. I would have thought she'd be feeling victorious on account of my father having accepted the position of VP of Media Relations, but whenever we happen to make eye contact, she seems more upset than ever.

•••••

Today before Family Life class, I told Missy Shoemaker that I'd gotten so good at my public speaking technique that I could now picture people not just in their underwear, but completely nude. I thought I was being pretty clever until she pointed out that half the people in the room were guys and that Lyle Filbender probably had hair on his genitals already. For the rest of the class, I couldn't visualize anything but Lyle's hairy groin, and as a consequence, I was unable to string more than two words together during my practice speech.

"Don't worry," said Mr. Bennet. "There's still a week to go before the meeting. Plenty of time to prepare."

•••••

I tried giving my speech again today. My team had prepared many excellent points that made a lot of sense when we discussed them as a group, but when I got up in front of the class I stuttered and stumbled so badly that Lyle Filbender burst out laughing and was sent from the room.

Mr. Bennet regarded me thoughtfully.

"You're obviously passionate about this issue," he said, "otherwise, you wouldn't have become so involved in it. Maybe you need to focus less on organized arguments and more on speaking from the heart. Tell me, is there one particular incident that really drew you to the cause?"

I pictured Daryl sitting by himself eating off an orange plastic tray and shrugged.

"Think about it," said Mr. Bennet. "It could be the key."

•••••

I called Daryl and told him about the problems I've been having with my speech.

"My teacher wants to know why this is so important to me," I said. "Of course I'm not going to tell him about you, but do you think it would be okay if I told him I have a friend who sometimes eats at the soup kitchen?" Daryl was agitated by the very suggestion, but after I promised that no one would ever suspect I was talking about him, he reluctantly agreed.

• • • • •

It worked! Today, when I stood in front of the class, I thought about Daryl and the words just came pouring out.

"You think this is just about crazy people with Cheez Whiz sandwiches in their pockets?" I concluded. "Well, it's not! I know someone, a boy my very own age, who eats breakfast at that soup kitchen just so he won't have to go to school hungry. You'd never think it to look at him, but it's true! So remember — the person who relies on the Holy Light Mission for his daily bread could be anyone. It could be the person on the street, or it could be the person sitting next to you. Someday, it could even be you."

I was so brilliant that I started to hyperventilate and Mr. Bennet made me breathe into a paper bag to prevent me from passing out. Later, he asked if I really knew a boy who eats breakfast at the Mission.

"Yes. No. Maybe. I'm not telling — you can't make me!" I blurted. Then I fled the room before he was able to break down my defenses and force a confession out of me.

• • • • •

I had a surprise session with my fine-looking psychologist, Dr. Anderson. Much of our discussion focused on what kinds of secrets are appropriate to keep, and what kinds should be shared with those in a position to help.

"Mr. Bennet told me you seemed very upset when he asked you about the mystery boy who eats at the soup kitchen," she said gently. "Do you realize that the school system offers support for families in crisis? If you have a friend in a difficult situation, you can tell me. I might be able to help."

She was so kind and logical and goodlooking that I felt my resolve to keep Daryl's secret slipping away.

"I was talking about myself," I admitted desperately. "I'm the mystery boy!" I confessed that my good-for-nothing father had driven the family business into the ground and that we were barely scraping by on my mother's measly part-time salary. "Please don't confront them about it," I begged. "They're terribly embarrassed by their inability to provide for me and I have no idea how they'll react if their ugly little secret is revealed to the world."

Dr. Anderson nodded slowly, thanked me for my remarkable candor and agreed to make no immediate attempt to confirm my outlandish story. She didn't cry in front of me, but I'm almost sure I saw a glint in her eye as I was leaving. It must hurt her to know how her favorite patient is suffering.

• • • • •

With the city council meeting just three days away, the Save Our Soup Kitchen contingent has been out in full force trying to encourage people to come down and fill the spectator seats.

"It's not enough for one or two people to give moving speeches," said Jerry, as pairs of volunteers filed out of the Mission to go knocking on doors. "City council needs to see that our supporters are willing to show up and be counted."

After everyone had left, I told Jerry that he'd hurt my feelings by suggesting that my moving speech

wasn't going to be enough to save the day. He laughed and said that he hoped it would be.

• • • • •

Ruth has guaranteed me forty-two warm bodies to fill seats at the city council meeting.

"They're all from my Gay Women for Social Responsibility organization," she explained excitedly. "I was bragging about what you've been up to lately, and they insisted on showing their support — for the soup kitchen *and* for you." She chortled. "They could hardly believe you were the same boy who nearly ate Mr. Juicy out of house and home at our last rally! What a difference a few months can make." I thanked Ruth and asked if she and Aunt Maud would be attending the city council meeting, too.

"We wouldn't miss it for the world," she promised.

• • • • •

This evening after supper I went into the den, closed the door and called my media contacts one last time to make sure they were going to show up at the meeting. The reporter with the tortoiseshell glasses said she'd be there, and so did the beautiful Lori Anderson of CTY television. My ex-overlord, Mr. Fitzgerald, on the other hand, complained about the fact that I was calling him at home again.

"But it really is an emergency this time!" I cried. "Do you realize that you have the opportunity to influence a decision that could affect hundreds of people? A little positive press could go a long way toward saving that soup kitchen and keeping hungry kids fed, you know." This last part seemed to get to him, because he grunted,

"I'll think about it." I thanked him, then asked if he'd had a chance to talk to his daughter about me. Unfortunately, we somehow got disconnected before I heard his reply.

When I came out of the den, BISOB's new VP of Media Relations asked who I'd been talking to. I walked past him without a word.

Let him make his own contacts.

• • • • •

Mr. Bennet and Miss Thorvaldson have decided to take the class down to city hall tomorrow to watch Lyle Filbender and me give our speeches. Lyle wasn't too happy when he heard the news, and neither was I. We complained that by putting our classmates in the audience, they had just turned up the heat in our pressure cooker about ten thousand degrees. Mr. Bennet apologized, but said it was too late to change plans because permission slips had already been sent home.

"This is all your fault," snarled Lyle as we headed back to our lockers. "My dad would *never* have made me do this if he hadn't found out you were doing it." He kicked my locker door so hard that several of my pin-up girls fluttered to the floor. "I'm going to get you for this," he said, jabbing a hairy finger in my face. "Just you wait."

• • • • •

I told Daryl and John Michael about Lyle's threat and suggested that they act as my personal bodyguards from now on. John Michael offered to teach me kickboxing so that I could defend myself instead, but I told him that surrounding myself with people whose lives were

dedicated to my personal safety was more in keeping with the image I had of myself.

"How about this?" asked Daryl, licking his finger and sticking it in my ear. "Is this in keeping with the image you have of yourself?"

"Not really," I admitted, trying in vain to wipe his saliva from my ear canal. I waited until his back was turned to sneak up and stick my licked finger in *his* ear, but I guess he heard me coming, because he whirled around, grabbed me and wrestled my slimy finger into my own ear instead. After a heroic tussle, I said that I knew when I was beaten and suggested that he go back to reading his magazine, which he did.

"So," I said, trying to sneak up on him again, "are you coming to the council meeting tomorrow?"

"I don't know," he replied, jerking my legs out from under me. "What do you need me there for?"

I thought of my vision — the one where he's all by himself, eating off an orange plastic tray. "Inspiration," I told him.

He said he'd think about it.

•••••

My mother just came in to say good-night and to hang my freshly ironed shirt in my closet.

"Nervous?" she asked, sitting down on the edge of my bed and smoothing out the comforter.

"Yes. No. I don't know." I shrugged, snuggling deeper under the covers.

She smiled and said how proud she was of me.

"Even if it means Grandmother hates us all forever?" I asked. She nodded. "Even if the Mission stays open and ruins the House of Toilets?" I asked. She nodded.

"Even if it destroys Dad's reputation in the business community and puts him out of a job? Even if we someday find ourselves unable to scrape together enough money to buy the necessities of life?"

My mother laughed. "Well, if you manage to save the soup kitchen, at least we'll have somewhere to eat, right?" She leaned over and kissed me on the forehead. "The fact is, honey, I'm proud of you *especially* because of those things. You're taking a risk by standing up for what you believe in, and that takes courage."

I thought about what she was saying, then asked, "Does that mean you think Dad is a coward?"

She shook her head and said she was proud of us both, but for different reasons.

A short while after she turned off the lights and left, I heard the door creak open. My father tiptoed across my bedroom floor and looked down at me for a long time, but I squeezed my eyes shut and pretended to be asleep, and eventually he left.

●●●●●

It's very late now. I was having some trouble sleeping, so I decided to say a prayer. I must say it was one of my best ever. In fact, I'm getting so good that I may have to reconsider my position as a godless heathen at some point.

"I'm sure You have plenty to eat up in heaven," I began. "But down here on earth, there are boys my very own age who will go to school hungry if the Holy Light Mission closes. Don't ask me to name names, because I won't — not even for You. It's not important, anyway — the important thing is that You pay attention to what's going on in the city council meeting tomorrow and do what You have to do to save our soup kitchen. And if, in Your eternal wisdom, You see fit to unleash Your wrath upon Lyle Filbender as a divine consequence for threatening me, I want You to know that I would consider it a personal favor. The end."

Well! After the Night of Marv, I promised God that I would stop asking for things like porn and reserve my prayers for matters of life and death and I guess I kept my promise, because if saving the Holy Light Mission isn't a matter of life and death, I don't know what is. Suddenly, I have a good feeling about tomorrow.

•••••

Last night? When I said I had a good feeling about today? What I actually meant was that I had a horrible feeling and that it was starting to eat holes into the lining of my stomach. The city council meeting starts in two hours. I just threw up three bowlfuls of Lucky Charms and I'm sweating like a pig. I don't think I can do this.

•••••

BANG! BANG! BANG!

My grandmother is at the bathroom door. She wants to get in — she says her girdle is hanging up on the towel rack and she can't get dressed without it.

That's funny. I didn't notice anything but towels hanging on the towel rack. Wait ... what's this ...?

Oh, god! *I've been wiping my brow with my grandmother's girdle!*

Excuse me. I think I'm going to be sick again.

•••••

My mother just left after ten fruitless minutes of trying to talk me out of the bathroom.

"Go away!" I shouted. "I'm not going to the council meeting!" She reminded me how proud she was of my courage. "You're going to have to go back to being proud of me for my looks!" I hollered. "Because I'm not coming out of here!"

•••••

What do you know? I'm out of there. And in five minutes, we leave for City Hall.

It was all my father's doing, if you can believe it — he climbed onto the kitchen roof and into the bathroom window while my mother distracted me at the door. I was furious when I turned around and saw him standing there, but in a very calm voice he said, "Son, put down your grandmother's girdle and let's talk." I hadn't even realized I was still clutching the girdle — that's how far gone I was! I dropped the cursed thing with a small shriek, and after I did, he sat down on the edge of the bathtub and apologized for everything.

"I was wrong," he said. "Things aren't more complicated when you're an adult. Sometimes adults just like to think they are because it makes it easier for us to do what we want to do instead of doing the right thing." He reached into his pocket and pulled out a crumpled letter. "My BISOB resignation," he said, waving it at me. "Effective immediately." For a long moment, he fingered the letter, frowning. "I'm not going to make you attend that meeting, son," he said at last, looking up. "But I want you to know that I'll be awfully proud to stand by your side if you decide to go."

What could I do? I let him give me a hug, then unlocked the bathroom door and gave my mother a hug. She laughed and hugged me back, then hugged my father, who hugged me again. It was such a frenzy of

hugging that I even hugged my grandmother until I noticed the look in her eyes.

"My ... girdle?" she breathed, flaring her nostrils at me. I gave her one last squeeze, hitched my thumb toward the bathroom floor and hurried off to get dressed.

•••••

WE WON! WE WON! WE WON!!

We did it — we really did it! Council's decided to include three years of funding for the Holy Light Mission in the new budget. It's a miracle!

To be honest, there were times when I had my doubts. It was very intimidating walking into city hall, and then the three agenda items before ours took nearly two hours. They were very boring compared to our important issue. Who cares about bilingual parking tickets? And how could anyone possibly think that building a five-star hotel for cats is more important than providing hot meals for actual human beings?

The longer the cat lady rambled on, the more ill I began to feel. I went to the bathroom at least a dozen times; I reread my speech until the words got blurry. The place was packed and tensions were running high. From across the room, Lyle Filbender made several rude gestures toward me before finally drawing his index finger across his throat, clearly indicating his intention to kill me! Alarmed, I jumped up to go inform Miss Thorvaldson of this threat to my person, but as I did so, Cat Woman wrapped it up, and council introduced our issue.

Jerry spoke first for our side. He was eloquent and passionate and did a very good job of articulating the need for a community soup kitchen. Marv spoke first for the other side. He frothed at the mouth a great deal and shook his cane in a menacing fashion at the Save Our Soup Kitchen section of the gallery.

Then it was my turn.

The walk to the podium was hideous, and when I got there, the microphone was way too high for me, so I had to stand there like a jerk while some lackey came over and adjusted it. Then I opened my mouth and my voice cracked so badly that it sounded like high-pitched speaker feedback. I swear I nearly bolted — my eyes actually darted around the room, looking for an emergency exit. That's when I spotted Daryl. He was alone at the very back of the room, half hidden in the shadow of a pillar. He didn't make any gestures of encouragement — I couldn't even tell if he was looking at me — but seeing him there reminded me why *I* was there, so I took a deep breath and started to speak.

I can't remember half of what I said, but I do know that I was at least a million times more inspiring than Lyle Filbender. He sounded like a defective robot in need of a battery change and had to be reprimanded twice for calling the Mission's clients "bums." Then, on the way down from the podium, he tripped and fell flat on his face. I knew it was a good sign — and I was right, because after Jerry and Marv gave their rebuttal speeches, the city councilors conferred for just a few short minutes before announcing the good news. Jerry closed his eyes and sank to his knees. The Gay Women for Social Responsibility leaped to their feet. Everyone else started shouting. Camera bulbs flashed, reporters fought their way through the crowd hoping for an exclusive. My mom and dad and Aunt Maud and Ruth surrounded me in a heartwarming group hug that lasted

right up until Janine clawed her way to my side, at which point I ditched them for the squeeze.

When the crowd thinned, I looked for Daryl, but he must have slipped out right after the verdict was read. Miss Thorvaldson came over and congratulated me, however, and even introduced me to her boyfriend. Mr. Loewen was small and pleasant-looking and kept his arm around her the whole time.

"She's really something, isn't she?" I asked, pumping his hand manfully as I beamed at Miss Thorvaldson.

"Yes, she is," he agreed with a smile.

Afterward, as we filed onto the bus to head back to school, I told Miss Thorvaldson that her boyfriend seemed nice and asked if she was serious about him. She told me it was none of my business and later gave me a detention when she overheard me entertaining my classmates by passionately kissing my gym bag and moaning, "Oh, Miss Thorvaldson! It is I, Mr. Loewen!"

Still! The city council meeting was quite an experience — and we won!

●●●●●

My parents picked up buckets and buckets of fried chicken for a celebration dinner at our place. They also ordered multiple large Styrofoam containers of every side dish on the menu and several bags of bite-sized brownies. The Sweetgrasses showed up, practically collapsing under the weight of fresh baked goodies from the Blue Moon Café, Daryl arrived carrying three bags of Doritos he'd probably lifted from Marv's gas station convenience store right before he got kicked out for good, and Jerry entered with a jumbo box of Twinkies under each arm. Oh, the bounty! It brought a lump to my throat that had nothing to do with the two tubs of gravy I single-handedly polished off in the orgy of consumption.

When dinner was over, we all sat in the living room and talked excitedly about the day's events. Daryl did such an excellent impression of Lyle Filbender falling on his face that the rest of us screamed with laughter. This got John Michael's little sister, Lucy, so keyed up that she started dancing around the room. My father cranked the stereo and we all got up to boogie — all except my grandmother, who had eaten heartily but in sullen silence.

As we were dancing around, Aunt Maud and Ruth suddenly announced that saving the soup kitchen wasn't the only exciting news we had to celebrate, because only hours earlier Aunt Maud had learned that she'd successfully conceived by artificial insemination. She and Ruth were going to be mothers! I jumped for joy until the fried chicken caught up with me and I slumped over, wheezing.

"Why are you wheezing?" I asked my grandmother, who was clutching the arm of the sofa as if for dear life. She gave me a shell-shocked look but didn't answer.

I guess we both need to lay off the fried chicken.

• • • • •

Today my classmates and I hardly talked about anything but my brilliant performance in front of council yesterday, and I must say, I've never enjoyed school so much. Janine was obviously warm for my form, but she had to get in line behind the rest of the honeys who wanted a piece of me.

"Calm down, ladies! There's plenty to go around," I

laughed, as I graciously accepted LifeSavers from a bashful Theodore Pinker, who passed them over without even licking them first. Lyle Filbender was so put off by my exploding popularity that he lunged at me during music class, tripped over a bongo drum and gave himself a bleeding nose, and right before the end of the day, Miss Thorvaldson heard Missy Shoemaker say that I'd done a pretty good job for a pubic lice with a two-inch doink and gave Missy a detention.

This was such a perfect day that I may suggest to my mother that I never go to school again. What would be the point? It's got to be all downhill from here.

• • • • •

My mother wasn't keen on my suggestion about dropping out, but that's okay, because on the way to school this morning, an old woman in a limp blue toque and filthy overcoat approached John Michael and me. It was Lydia, one of the soup kitchen regulars. For a long moment, she just stared at me with watery eyes. Then she blurted, "Hey. Ain't you that kid what saved Jerry's place?" When I nodded, she gave me a broad, crack-lipped smile, waved half a sandwich at me and continued on her way.

My popularity extends past Joe Average to the very fringes of society. Hooray!

• • • • •

My grandmother dismantled the War Room this evening. My mother says she's relieved to have the dining room back, and my father says they'll have to get someone in to repair the dents my grandmother's wooden mallet made in the surface of the dining room table, but I feel rather sorry for her. Without a cause to fight for — or a cherished grandson to spoil rotten — she seems rather lost.

Perhaps I should offer to let her treat me to a meal of barbequed ribs.

• • • • •

The principal of my school decided to surprise me with a community service award in order to recognize my dedication to the soup kitchen cause! There was an assembly in the gym today — the beautiful Lori Anderson of CTY television was there, and so was the reporter with the tortoiseshell glasses. The principal introduced me and led the student body in a round of applause. Then, after handing me a lovely gold-embossed certificate, he passed the microphone to a very startled Miss Thorvaldson.

"You've had the pleasure of his presence in your class all year long, Enid," he chuckled, with one eye on the camera. "Who better to say a few words about this fine, upstanding young man?"

Miss Thorvaldson looked so ill that I wondered if she, too, had a pathological fear of public speaking. It took a long moment of twitching and fidgeting with the collar of her gorgeous cable-knit turtleneck before she was able to pull herself together and begin.

"A little louder, please," I murmured through my dazzling smile. "I think the people in the back are having a hard time hearing you." She gritted her teeth and continued, and although her speech was extremely short, I was so touched by the kind things she said that it hardly bothered me at all when she refused to give me a hug at the end of my assembly.

Tape #3

· · · · ·

Well, I've been doing a lot of thinking these past few days, and I've decided that this is the perfect place to end my childhood recordings. I'm running out of tape, and besides, I've just fought an epic battle and won — practically single-handedly. What a terrific chapter this is going to make in my best-selling memoirs someday! And by springboarding directly from this pinnacle to adulthood, I will avoid subjecting my readers to any of the potential awkwardness that may yet await me as I claw my way to full maturity. Things like pimples and braces, growth spurts and voice changes. First dates — first girlfriends — first sexual encounters! While I obviously feel confident in my ability to carry myself through these situations with grace and aplomb, there is always the outside chance that I will falter in some small way. And although the responsibility for making me look bad will almost certainly fall squarely on the shoulders of some insensitive boor, I still think it's better that my loyal readers are left with the lingering image of my youthful self as a celebrated hero who —

END TAPE

THREE DAYS LATER...

I remembered Jerry's laugh,
and the way he'd hand out
instant coffee at the door of
the Mission on bitter cold days
and worry about the people that
everyone else had forgotten.

I got a new tape ... I ... I just had to. I'm so upset I didn't know what I might say otherwise — or who I might say it to.

I can't believe it.

They shut down the Mission. They shut it down! Those ... those *bastards*!

I'd just picked up a cream puff pastry at the Blue Moon Café and was heading up to 7-Eleven for a Slurpee when I walked by the Mission and noticed a big padlock on the door. I didn't think anything of it at first, but when I went closer, I saw a sign that said, "Closed Due to Lack of Funding." I thought it was a joke — or a mistake. I mean, how could it not be a joke or mistake? They promised Jerry his funding. They *promised*.

But it wasn't a joke or a mistake. When I looked in the grimy window of the Holy Light Mission, the place was empty.

I ran back to the Blue Moon Café and burst inside, shouting, "Mrs. Sweetgrass! Mrs. Sweetgrass!" Before she could answer, Jerry walked in. Apparently, he'd just been up at my house looking for me.

"I wanted you to hear it from me," he said. "We lost our funding — all of it. Someone got to a couple of swing vote city councilors, and they refused to vote in favor of the budget until our funding was taken out. I guess the others figured it was such a small line item that it wasn't worth holding up the budget over." He rubbed the back of his hand across his forehead. "We were already overextended and we hadn't made rent in two months, so when the landlord heard that we'd lost our funding, he padlocked the door." Jerry sighed and put his hand on my shoulder. "Try not to feel too upset. We did the best we could."

I stared at him, then gave a violent shrug. "WHO GIVES A SHIT?" I shouted, smacking his hand away. "PEOPLE CAN'T EAT OUR BEST FOR BREAKFAST!"

Then, with my throat feeling so tight I could hardly breathe, I bolted from the café and now here I am, barricaded in my room. And I'm not going anywhere — or doing anything — ever again. What would be the point in a world where hungry children aren't worth holding up budgets for?

•••••

My mother didn't try to make me go to school today, which is good, because I wouldn't have gone, anyway. I spent the whole day lolling in bed with a pillow over my head and didn't eat one single bite off the trays my mother brought up. She loaded them with my favorites — pancakes and breakfast sausages, fried peanut butter sandwiches and chocolate Ding Dongs — but quite frankly, the sight of all that food just made me ill.

•••••

My father and I have called everyone we can think of, but no politicians are available for comment and the media is not returning phone calls.

The Holy Light Mission is yesterday's news.

•••••

John Michael came by the house after school today to see if I was okay, but I made my mother send him away. I would have made her send Daryl away, too, but he never came by.

•••••

I haven't eaten, watched TV or changed my pajamas in

three days. My parents were so concerned that they asked my fine-looking psychologist, Dr. Anderson, to make a house call.

"This really isn't necessary," I announced, as she sat down on the couch across from me. "Sure, I'm upset, but with the closure of the soup kitchen, don't you think there are kids out there who might need your help more than I do?" She tried to tell me that my problems were just as important as theirs, but I told her that was a load of malarkey and that as far as I was concerned, our sessions together were over.

"Well, let's see how you feel in a couple of weeks," she suggested gently, as she pulled on her coat and got ready to leave. "By the way, my sister asked me to pass along her condolences. She was really rooting for you guys."

"Your sister?" I yawned, scratching my belly.

"Yes, Lori — the television journalist from CTY."

Somehow, this penetrated the fog of my despair. I slowly rolled off the couch and followed Dr. Anderson to the door. "You never told me you had a sister," I said, feeling slightly hurt.

"Actually, I have two of them," she replied, heading down the front steps. "We're triplets."

You have got to be kidding me.

• • • • •

This evening my grandmother came into the TV room and said it was time I stopped feeling sorry for myself. She said I was making far too big a deal out of what had happened, especially considering the fact that as heir to the House of Toilets fortune, I was going to personally benefit from the improved business climate the community was going to enjoy now that the Mission was gone. "Try to look on the bright side," she encouraged.

"This will probably help motivate some of those people to get jobs so that they won't *need* a soup kitchen."

She stood tall and still and silent, waiting for me to respond. When I didn't, she plumped down on the couch beside me and heaved a noisy sigh.

"In case you're wondering, I had nothing to do with the shenanigans that went on behind the scene after that dang meeting," she said. I looked at her for the first time, and she hesitated before continuing in a voice that was just the tiniest bit softer. "Whippersnapper, you may think me a selfish, unfeeling old bat, but I play by the rules and you won fair and square. I won't pretend to like where you're coming from — and I can't honestly say that I even respect it — but I am sorry you got done such a dirty turn, and ... and I'm willing to let bygones be bygones if you are."

I didn't really want to let bygones be bygones, but as I listened to my grandmother speak, I suddenly realized how badly I wanted things between us to go back to the way they'd always been, so I shrugged and reminded her that I've always been partial to a good rib dinner.

"Well, what are we waiting for!" she cried, slapping her hands against her knees in a pleased sort of way. I shuffled to my feet, feeling hungry for the first time in days, and as I edged past her to go upstairs and get dressed, she wordlessly wrapped her arms around me and squeezed. It felt nice.

●●●●●

My grandmother packed her bags and flew back to Florida on the first flight out this morning.

"For better or worse, my work here is done — for now," she declared as she watched my father drag her steamer trunks down the front steps and load them into the waiting cab. "But you may all rest assured that I'll be back when that unwed lesbian daughter of mine brings forth issue. Mother, have mercy on us all! I hardly know what the world is coming to these days." My parents both rolled their eyes, but I said, "No need to worry, Grandmother. Although my gay partner and I didn't cope at all well with the demands of raising our beloved son, Henry, Aunt Maud and Ruth clearly have the kind of loving and supportive relationship that is ideal for nurturing children." I don't think she was very comforted by my words, because she gave a great huff and sailed down the steps to the cab. As she was arranging herself in the back of it, I leaned in the open window, told her that I loved her and asked if she was going to let my father keep running the House of Toilets flagship store.

"What choice do I have?" she sighed. "Profits are up eighteen percent. Money talks."

With that, she ordered the cab to the airport and was gone.

• • • • •

I finally felt strong enough to return to school today. It seemed like everyone had heard about Jerry losing his funding. It was very embarrassing. If people weren't treating me like a leper, they were asking if I'd be giving back my community service award, since the soup kitchen ended up closing, after all. I told the vast majority of them to bugger off and mind their own business, but later, I snuck the gold-embossed cardboard certificate out of my locker, ripped it into tiny pieces and stuffed the pieces down one of the toilets in the boys' bathroom. I was feeling pretty sorry for myself, and I guess even

 Tape #4

Miss Thorvaldson shared my sentiment, because when the toilet later flooded and the janitor produced the irrefutable evidence of my complicity, she didn't even give me a detention.

The biggest surprise, however, was the fact that Lyle Filbender didn't heckle me once all day. Touched by this unprecedented display of consideration for my feelings, I took a moment at dismissal time to wearily congratulate Lyle on taking his first, lurching step toward civilized humanity. Twenty minutes later I retracted my kind compliment when, as John Michael and I were walking home, Lyle and his gang of Junior BISOB thugs jumped out from behind a pile of junk in the empty lot beside the boarded-up Mission. They knuckle-walked their way over to where we were standing and stood on the sidewalk in front of us, blocking our path.

"So," sneered Lyle, grinning at his posse as he gave me a sharp shove in the shoulder. "Who's the big man now?"

John Michael instinctively moved closer in order to protect me, but I gently pushed him aside. I thought about Lyle's question and the many excellent responses I could give.

Then I hoofed him in the nuts as hard as I could.

"I am," I replied, as I watched him writhe on the dirty sidewalk. "Come on, John Michael," I said. "Let's go see if your mom has any day-old pecan pie left."

John Michael nodded wordlessly, Lyle's baboons parted like the Red Sea, and we continued on our way.

●●●●●

I haven't talked to Daryl since the Mission shut down. I saw him the other day, talking to some of the squeegee kids who were working the boulevard in front of Marv's gas station, but I ducked behind a building when he looked over in my direction. I just don't know what to say to him.

•••••

We had Jerry over for dinner tonight. He's going to a soup kitchen in Medicine Hat, Alberta. When I expressed surprise that he'd found another job so quickly, he laughed.

"There's no shortage of jobs out there for someone like me," he said, helping himself to another Salisbury steak. "In fact, this will be my fourth mission in three years." He explained that his other missions had all shut down — just like the Holy Light Mission. "There are lots of reasons, but most of them have to do with funding." He chewed the rubbery meat thoughtfully, swallowed with difficulty and added, "What it comes down to, I suppose, is the fact that many of the people who are in the best position to help think that the problem has nothing to do with them."

After dinner, he thanked my parents and me for everything and gave us each a hug. "Keep up the good work," he said to me as he was leaving.

I smiled and said that I'd have to check my schedule. Then I wished him good luck and waved good-bye.

•••••

This weekend I walked by the boarded-up Mission for the first time since Jerry left town. There was a new sign on the door — this one said, "Coming Soon: Carl's Pawnshop." I stared at it for a long time. The last winds of winter were blowing old newspapers around, and the streets were empty, except for the squeegee kids.

 Tape #4

Watching them rattle their nearly empty tins at passing vehicles, I wondered if they were hungry. And I remembered Jerry's laugh, and the way he'd hand out instant coffee at the door of the Mission on bitter cold days and worry about the people that everyone else had forgotten.

•••••

Last night while I was flipping through one of my old porn magazines, my mother knocked on the door and poked her head into my bedroom. I'm quite sure she saw the glossy spread of the little blond vixen in the baby doll pajamas before I was able to shove the magazine under my pillow, but she didn't say anything about it. Instead, she sat down at the edge of my bed and told me yet again how proud she was of me.

"Yes, well, that doesn't really help anybody, does it?" I asked impatiently, itching to get back to my vixen.

"No, I don't suppose it does," she said slowly. "But ... what if I said you could invite a friend over for meals, anytime you want? Would that help?" Before I could answer, she continued, "Sometimes we can't save the day, honey. Sometimes all we can do is make a difference, one person at a time."

I thought about what she was saying. It didn't exactly fit with the image I have of myself as a vastly influential crusader and media darling, but somehow it made sense.

I thanked her and, after she left, returned to my vixen.

Hours later, I turned off the light and slept soundly for the first time in weeks.

Finally, I had something to say to Daryl.

•••••

I went to Daryl's place right after school this afternoon.

The whole way over, I rehearsed what I was going to say to him, but when I arrived, I got a sudden attack of nerves, so I sat down on an old tire in his front yard and did deep-breathing exercises. Unfortunately, he happened to look out of his living room window and notice me sitting there. Sneaking out his back door, he tiptoed up behind me and shouted, "BOO!" as loud as he could. I was so startled that I toppled backward into the tire and it was just like old times as Daryl leaped on top of me, shouting and bouncing my poor backside against the cold, wet ground. When he finally got tired, he plopped down beside me and said, "So." I said, "So," back, and then, before my courage failed me, asked him if he'd like to come to my place for breakfast.

"When?" he asked.

"Well ... every day," I replied. "My mom said it would be okay." Daryl looked upset when I said this, but I quickly clarified that she didn't know anything about anything. "She just said I could invite a friend over for meals if I wanted," I explained. "That's all." When he still didn't say anything, I added, "We always have a couple of boxes of Lucky Charms kicking around, you know."

After a short silence, Daryl gave me a long, sideways glance. "Well," he said, shrugging like it was no big deal to him one way or the other. "Lucky Charms *are* delicious."

"Magically!" I grinned, throwing my arm across his shoulders.

With a grunt, he gave me a jab in the ribs and told me to stop acting like a nimrod, then invited me inside to dry off.